VENUS FIGURINES
The Persuasion of Anya

ROY CHESNUT

Cover Design by: Ryan McCarron

Full Moon Publishing, LLC
Glade Spring, VA
Fullmoonpublishingllc.com

ISBN: 1946232432
ISBN-13: 978-1946232434

Dedicated to Nadine Chesnut, mi esposa.

CONTENTS

Inspired by 'Love in the Time of Cholera' by Gabriel Garcia Marquez.

FORWARD

Venus Figurines is a love story written as a modern myth. It is about Anya and James whose struggle with love becomes obsessive, ritualistic, and self-defining. The underlying theme of my story is how love drives the creation of art, particularly the art of a venerating woman – Venus Art. Venus Art is very old. Some ancient examples are statuettes of women carved from mammoth ivory by Neolithic people thousands of years ago. Archaeologists call these artifacts Venus Figurines. Although we can only speculate about what motivated these ancient sculptors, I believe they were inspired by love and beauty, as were the myths and artwork of Venus that came later. Enjoy my book.

CHAPTER 1

He placed her dainty foot into the palm of his warm, brown hand. Her foot was ill at ease in his hand as if held against its will. He ran his fingers over it, caressing the contour of her ankle and the shape of her unblemished sole, all of which came together in his mind with a space and gravity all their own.

It tickled and she crinkled her nose. Her reflexes flinched, betraying aversion to his touch. "Relaxxxssss," Feo hissed, grinning at her with gold teeth. The skull tattoo on his shoulder leered at her innocence, eyelessly.

Anya could not bear to look at his pockmarked face or rough hands as they touched her smooth skin. She turned away from him in dread, scanning the dirt-caked windows and concrete floor of the studio in search of solace, her gaze coming to rest on the soiled sheets of an unmade bed.

"How much?" James interrupted their strange communion.

Feo turned his head towards James and said, "For her foot?"

"No, everything."

Feo petted her calve while inhaling her perfume and anxiety. "I have to think about it." He shaped his hand into a caliper with his thumb and index finger and slid it up her lower leg. His spidery caress made goose bumps rise on her helpless flesh. She felt like a fly in his web, but relented and endured his touch anyway.

Sitting perched beside James, aloft on a white sofa, she looked like an angel on a cloud or a porcelain miniature on a cake. They looked down at Feo, who knelt in silence. James nudged her. She glanced at him hesitantly, but then relented and while nodding 'yes', lifted her dress further, succumbing to circumstances that were beyond her control. Feo's hands climbed to her knee and slid along her thigh.

"Sixty thousand," Feo blurted out.

"Are you kidding? I was thinking more like forty. How about forty, Feo? Think forty."

James glanced at Anya, who looked ashamed. Beads of sweat formed on her upper lip. She shot a despairing look back at James, which seemed to ask, 'Must we go through with this?' She held his hand, feeling for the protection of his love.

"That's an insult! Sixty thousand?"

"Fifty."

"You are trying to steal from me, *gringo*." Feo, opaque behind his dark glasses, lit a cigarette and blew smoke rings at James with relaxed aplomb.

Anya's face glistened with fear. The dull throb of regret beat in her chest. James fanned the smoke with a hand while he waited, but Feo betrayed nothing. "Well, is it fifty?" James asked.

Feo's glasses peered away blindly, as if distracted. "I have many other things I can do with my time, *cabrón*. Sixty thousand." His Mexican brogue colored his speech with melodrama. Smoke billowed from his nostrils and devolved into fairies in Anya's imagination. She thought of a Minotaur wearing dark glasses and jeans, with black hair and tattoos who exhaled angelic spirits with angel wings, some blowing trumpets.

"Fifty-five," James replied. He could easily afford more, but his ego stopped him there.

Feo shook his head and then placed her foot on his chest over his heart and murmured, as though reciting a prayer, "To capture her soul. Isn't that what you want? What are you willing to pay for that?" Time slowed to a pause, standing still, while the gravity of his meaning sank in. He added, "For *that*, I need inspiration."

"What is he talking about?" Anya whimpered as her pores opened involuntarily, taking in the ambience of the moment, allowing it to mingle with her own, intimate chemistry. She felt violated.

Feo tapped his lips and waited in silence.

"So, you'll do it?" James asked, his face slick with dread.

"Sixty," Feo repeated. "I will think about it." He pushed his chair to one side. He was done for now.

"Did we just agree to something?" James was confused.

"There is no agreement." A woman's voice startled Anya and James. Isabella had been out of sight watching them, listening in; the sneaky voyeur that she was. Feo grinned, but Anya and James were horrified.

"You both look so guilty," Isabella said, slyly smirking. Anya glowed with embarrassment and looked away. Isabella was Feo's first cousin. She was also his lawyer and business manager.

Feo said, "We are all guilty and we will all suffer for it. You might ask yourself, Anya, how you came to be here, now, at this moment. What was the chain of events that led you here? What is the first link in the chain? What were the choices you made? How will the choice you make today affect your life tomorrow? I think you already know that there is no going back." His ticklish hand burned on her thigh, but she was helpless and could do nothing.

He continued, "And if you are wrong and this is a bad idea, it might bring you unhappiness for so long a time you will begin to think the only happiness you know is the happiness you used to know."

"Feo! What are you saying? Are you trying to talk her out of it?" James snapped.

Feo stopped speaking, but it was too late. What had been said had already been heard by Anya, whose thoughts turned inward, burrowing down inside to a place where they became images; images of naked girls showering in a locker room: a painful event from middle school. She was twelve.

After gym each day, the girls were required to shower. This meant they had to completely undress. They modestly wrapped themselves in towels and marched solemnly to the shower where they dropped the towels and joined the other naked nymphets in the spray and steam, giddy and pink with embarrassment. The gym teacher stood by the line of girls, ticking their names off a list as they passed, making it impossible to escape the appalling ritual. Anya called it the Shower of Mortification.

The Shower of Mortification distressed Anya to her core, but she endured each day with stoic grace and dignity. She would wait until all the girls had left before disrobing. As she removed her shoes and socks, and then shirt and pants, pangs tickled her belly. She undressed until she stood in nothing but a bra and underwear. She then wrapped herself in a towel beneath which she wriggled off her undergarments, revealing nothing to the outside world.

One day, as she walked with dignified resignation, from locker to shower, she noticed the closet door move. As she passed, the door flew open. She turned and saw the janitor's pink, domed head staring at her from the closet. His mouth hung open exposing brown, jagged teeth and bleeding gums. She shrieked and in her panic, dropped the towel which gave him a full frontal view of her nude body — an image that he greedily supped up with his burning blue eyes. He licked his greasy lips as though he had just swallowed something sweet. The nymphets all began to scream, the gym teacher blew her whistle, and pandemonium ensued.

The next thing she remembered was sitting in the principal's office, where she was forced to recount each moment of the indignity to the principal, her father, and a police officer. She spoke with a broken voice as she relived it in front of them. The humiliation etched into her soul, leaving a scar. She was convinced the janitor would forever be able to recall the vision of her nude body in his mind at will, whenever he liked, holding her captive, permanently violating her privacy. He had stolen from her the first tiny bit of virtue and she felt degraded. She refused to shower at school again.

James touched Anya, who returned from her thoughts to find that she was still sitting in Feo's studio. They all looked at her as though waiting for a reply to Feo's question, which she could scarcely recall. It was something about unhappiness and persistent regret. She turned to James, whom she loved and trusted, and for whom she was willing to do whatever it took to cure him of his obsession and suffering. James, in spite of burning with jealousy at the sight of Feo touching her, reassured her with a nod and a smile.

"Yes, I will do it," she said, relenting again as she had at each juncture in the past, agreeing to the next step in a slow sacrifice.

CHAPTER 2

After this first, painful meeting with Feo, James and Anya waited outside Feo's studio for Uber to pick them up and take them to his home in the Marina. The night was dark and damp and streetlights reflected off the slick sidewalk. They were south of Market in San Francisco, near Third and Bryant, in an industrial barrio of parking garages, auto repair shops, corrugated aluminum, and graffiti. Invisible to them, beyond the boundary of their mutual captivation, laid an eyesore of blight and soaking wet cardboard boxes that sheltered filthy, bearded men who shivered in the cold. One peered at them through a hole in his box.

The session with Feo churned in her mind. Despite feelings of moral degradation, her body responded to Feo's touch in ways that she could not admit, even to herself. Being watched by James while being touched by Feo heightened her sense of shame and spawned in her a new feral chemistry that took her against her will and brewed inside her, next to but separate from her sacred love for James. She shivered from it.

As they waited, her red hair absorbed moisture from the air and fanned out across her shoulders. "Oh, darn, my hair," she said and gathered it together, pulling it back into a ponytail.

"I love your hair like this — all frizzy. Let it loose," he said.

She did and it tumbled from her head, down her back in riplets of red, releasing a redolence he inhaled. It infected his blood, sedating him, easing his rage over the touching of her. He could not resist running his fingers through her hair. She laid her head on his shoulder. He wrapped her in his arms and touched her forehead with his lips. In the cool solitude of the damp night air, they began to relax.

In spite of their returning calm, the traumatic experience forced James to re-examine why they had come to see Feo in the first place. He asked himself two questions; questions he asked himself almost every daily: *Why am I here? What am I doing?*

He could stop the events set in motion, but even if he did, he would never be able to stop himself, so it was futile to try. Bringing Anya to Feo was just a symptom of his problem. James understood Feo's warning about making choices and recalled his own chain of events. He even remembered the first link in the chain. It was when he was very young; around three years. He remembered it well.

He and his parents, John and Vivian, lived in an apartment in Palo Alto near the hospital where Vivian was finishing her medical residency. John, a wealthy heir, did not work. He was sort of a house dad. Vivian's career provided the rhythm for their lives with each day neatly carved into discrete activities: John taking James to school while she went to the hospital. Dinners were prepared and served, laundry done, beds made, sheets changed, all forming a neat order of events. It was his mother's influence.

Since John did not have to work, he had not pursued a career. In fact, he had not pursued much of anything. He did collect stamps and was proud of his knowledge of them and of knowing the word

8

'philately', which he would rhyme with Lady Chatterley to impress his friends. For years, he unwittingly called himself a phillaterer, until a friend embarrassed him by telling him that, "A philatelist collects stamps; a phillaterer is someone who fellates." Sadly, philately was about as deep as things ever got for John. To his credit, he had not disintegrated into hedonism like his father, although the temptation was always tugging at his sleeve.

One night, the family watched a Western on television in the living room. James played on the rug with trucks, mostly ignoring the program. The Western climaxed and the commotion caught his attention. He turned to the TV just as one cowboy shot another, who fell to the ground.

"Well, he's dead," John said.

"Cowboy dead?" James said with surprise. At three, he knew that death was the end of life and that all of the dinosaurs had died before having baby dinosaurs so they were extinct. He knew that a dead body disappeared into dust and understood that the transition to dust happens because tiny bugs called germs eat the body and poop dust.

He dreamed about his conception of death. The death dream always began the same way as he drifted off to sleep, starting with weird sensations like dizziness or the feeling that he had shrunk in size or floated over the bed. As he shrank, the crack between the bed and the wall grew, drawing him in until he teetered over the edge and fell. He then drifted slowly downward into darkness until he landed softly on a pile of hay in a dimly lit tunnel with a concrete floor and red brick walls. John and Vivian were there. They were going somewhere. They asked him to hold their hands, but he would not and instead defiantly chewed on a plastic toy airplane. His parents told him to stop chewing on the plane, but he ignored them. Their facial expressions became flat and their voices emotionless and alien, as though they were in a trance.

He walked next to them through the tunnel, which turned a corner and then became bright with light. Steps led upward into a nursery school classroom and he could see books and toys. As they climbed the steps, he collapsed on the stairs, overcome with fatigue. His parents continued to climb the stairs, ignoring him. Then he died and turned to dust, a ball of lint; *Germ Poop.*

The transformation into Germ Poop was painless and he could still see and hear even though he was dead. He saw a second dust ball. They played together. That was how the dream ended.

The death of the cowboy startled James. He let go of his toys and stared at the TV, thinking about what he had just seen. He knew death happened to dinosaurs, but that did not mean that it happened to people. He planned to live forever.

He looked at his mother and asked, "Cowboy dead?"

"Yes, the cowboy is dead because back then cowboys shot each other, but these are not cowboy times. You'll never be shot by a cowboy."

James grasped the terrible truth about cowboy times. They were dangerous and you could die then. He was glad he was not a cowboy. He went back to his trucks, confident that he would live forever.

Shortly afterwards, he learned that everything dies. The journey from immortality to knowing that everything dies began in the middle of the night. On that night, the phone rang. It disturbed his sleep, but did not awaken him entirely. He heard his father exclaim, "Oh, my god! Oh, my god! I'll be right there." The urgency in his father's voice startled James. He sat up in bed and listened.

"What is it, John? What's the matter?" Vivian asked.

"It's mother. They found her lying in the hallway. She wasn't breathing. She's at the hospital. I have to go."

"Oh, John, I'm sorry."

After a long pause, John said, with a faltering voice, "Well, it's not as though it wasn't unexpected."

"Yes, I know."

"She would have been eighty-two, in December."

"A long life."

"Yeah, long enough. She had a full life, perhaps too full a life. I have to go to the house. I have to make the arrangements. Please, stay here with James."

"Of course."

James did not comprehend. He rolled over and fell back to sleep.

The next day, James played on the rug in the living room, encircled by toy trucks, soldiers, and planes. The television was on, tuned to Sesame Street. Vivian and John appeared. They settled on the couch. John switched off the television and said, "James."

James ignored him and continued to carefully stand soldiers in a toy dump truck while muttering make-believe to himself.

"James," John repeated in a louder, more serious voice. "James, look at Daddy."

"No."

"No? And what exactly do you mean by 'no,' young man?"

"No! I not looking at you, Daddy... I busy."

"Busy?" John affectionately tackled James onto the rug, who giggled as they tumbled. John sat up and pulled James into his lap. "James, I have something sad to tell you."

James continued playing with a soldier he held in his hand.

"Something happened to Geegee. Something sad." 'Geegee' meant grandmother; John's mother.

James turned and looked John in the eye for a surprised moment and said, "What happen to Geegee?"

"She died."

"No, Daddy. Geegee no die" James waited for his father to deny that she had died, and when he did not he shouted defiantly, "NO, DADDY!" He pushed his father's face away. "NO, DADDY, GEEGEE NO DIE." He twisted out of his father's lap and stood, stamping his foot on the floor, repeating, "NO, DADDY! NO, DADDY! GEEGEE NO DIE."

John and Vivian sat helplessly while they watched their son's psychic pain. All they could do was shed tears. James' stamping foot grew into a dance of hysterical grief. His red face glistened with tears and anger. He howled as he hadn't the words to properly express his shock and horror. He cried and cried and cried - for at least an hour, non-stop, pausing only to breathe, until he became exhausted and the crying faded away.

"Come see Daddy," John said and got down on his knees and held out his arms.

"NO, DADDY," James started crying again and ran away, across the living room where he stopped and turned and faced his father, glowering at him, angry over the truth he had revealed. "DADDY, GO AWAY!"

"He's freaked. I don't know what to do," John said.

Vivian took over. She opened her arms for him and said, "Come here, my James. Come see Mommy."

"MOMMIEEEEEEEEEEEEEEEEE!" he wailed, mouth opened wide,

drooling, his face swollen with grief. He danced with anger across the room. She picked him up.

"Shh, Shh, Shh, James. Mommy loves you."

"NO, MOMMIEEEEEEEEEEEEE!" he shrieked and swung his hand at her.

"He's hysterical," she said.

"Should we take him to the hospital?"

"No, he'll get over it. How about a teaspoon of wine?"

"Good idea, Doc," John disappeared and then returned with a bottle of port and a teaspoon. "This is sweet. He should like it." He gave them to Vivian, who administered the medicine to a cautious James. The port was strong. It burned his mouth and caught in his throat. He choked and began to cry again. Saliva, red with wine, trickled down his chin and across her arm.

"Oh, James, please calm down." She rocked him as he calmed. In a few minutes, he was quiet, his only sound being short bursts of reflexive sniffling. He fell asleep. The horror of death gradually ebbed away, but was never quite forgotten, always lurking, reminding him of the shortness of life and the problem of what to do while waiting for the end.

CHAPTER 3

James and Anya met at the City Lights Bookstore in San Francisco months before their visit to Feo's studio. On that night, just before they met, James sat in a sidewalk café on Columbus Boulevard near Chestnut Street. It was twilight in early summer. A marine layer cooled the evening. The clang of cable car bells punctuated the background din of the city. He sat alone, stirring an espresso with a spoon, while thumbing through *San Francisco Weekly* magazine, looking for things to do. He found nothing.

He had nowhere to go and nothing to do. Having nothing to do was a persistent problem for James. He had inherited a large trust fund and did not have to work for a living, so instead of struggling to survive, he struggled to fill his time. He did have a small business, which was buying and selling rare guitars. He bought them at estate sales and auctions and then sold them online and at fairs. The business took a few hours a week. It was a leisurely business — a gentlemen's business — almost a hobby; part time and modestly profitable.

Of all the problems one might have, being wealthy and idle is not exactly a tragedy, but still, James cursed his ennui each day. He could do nothing about it. He lacked the will, commitment, and talent to change his life, so, he lived dreading the present tense, which right now, passed by so slowly that he could count each momentito with a stir of his coffee spoon. He looked around at the others in the café to see how they passed their time. There was a bald man with a scab on his scalp slurping soup, two women with menus twittering at each other like birds, a couple who held hands and stared into each other's eyes, making James feel alone, reminding him of the Prufrock he'd become. He had withdrawn from life and avoided friends for weeks after his latest relationship disintegrated in public. As he sat in the café, he recalled the event. He and Janet, his girlfriend of seven weeks, met his best friend, Jack Hooker, and Jack's date for dinner over a month ago. They were late. James and Janet began to bicker over how he had parked the car while Jack and his date looked on.

"Sorry we're late," Jack sheepishly apologized.

"You took forever to park!" Janet said with a strained, angry voice.

"Jeez! Sorry. I wanted a close space. You know, to save some walking."

"We spent twenty minutes looking for a parking space!"

"Hey, try and relax. It was only seventeen minutes."

"Twenty minutes, seventeen minutes. Who cares? The point is it took WAY TOO LONG."

"Well, I'm sorry if I am not just like you, taking the first spot that you see, regardless of anything."

"WE SAVED A COUPLE OF BLOCKS! ARE YOU OUT OF YOUR MIND? Your parking habit – no, it's not a habit; I'm being kind to call it a habit — it's an impulse and it's not just with parking. It's with everything that you do! It's out of control!"

"I don't get what you mean," he lied. He had heard it before. He did dilly-dally, but then he thought, *She just doesn't understand the true meaning of having too much time on your hands.*

"IT'S A DISEASE. YOU NEED A SHRINK!" she shouted.

"I HAVE A SHRINK, AND HE THINKS I'M OKAY!" he shouted back.

A sullen silence followed. Finally, she said, "I can't stand it anymore," and left.

He did not miss her at all, but the breakup humiliated him. He withdrew to clear his head and assess his life, but after weeks of introspection, he had discovered nothing and gotten nowhere.

As the recollection faded, he found himself back in the café, starring at an obituary in *San Francisco Weekly*. He read the obit aloud, "Her name was Alice Smith, fifty-five. She had breast cancer. She was survived by her husband and two sons." He stopped. The few facts of her life made her death too real for him and grief, followed by dread, infected his mood. He began to feel nauseous. He had to leave, to get away. He dropped the tabloid, left cash for his bill, and fled down Columbus Boulevard, passing Joe DiMaggio Park and shops selling flowers. He picked his way between cars and pedestrians that hurried by, all rushing somewhere, each with a goal and purpose. Something he lacked. He felt vague envy toward them.

When he came to City Lights Bookstore, he took his eyes off the sidewalk and glanced through the bookstore window. He noticed an audience gathered 'round a man who was reading aloud. With his attention away from the sidewalk, he did not see the ragged bum crouched down below the ambience of the crowded sidewalk, leaning against a newspaper dispensary. James stumbled over him and lost his balance. They made eye contact. The bum said, "Don't do it! No, don't do it!"

James looked into the soiled face of the dirty beggar. "Don't do what?"

"Buy me a sandwich."

Now that's original! He considered rewarding the bum for his creative food pitch by hustling him into a sandwich shop and buying him all he could eat, plus food to go. Then, he recalled a glint of red in the audience at the bookstore. *What was that? Red hair? A woman?*

He forgot about the bum and looked again through the bookstore window. He saw Anya's red hair. A poster outside advertised a poetry reading, which was underway. He entered the bookstore, joined the crowd standing in the back, and scanned the audience. After spotting her, he moved to a position where he could see her more clearly.

She had curls the color of sunset that fell in ringlets to her shoulders. Her eyebrows knitted in relaxed concentration as she focused on the poetry being read aloud. She wore glasses and looked bookish, like 'Madam Librarian'. James glanced at the poet and found him boring, so he returned his attention to Anya's waterfall of hair, porcelain cheeks, full pink lips, and blue eyes. He could see the profile of her delicate shoulders and slender arms and wondered at what lay beneath her earth-tone sweater.

He had to meet her, to speak with her, to find out who she was. He returned to the back of the room — behind the audience — and waited.

When the reading ended, Anya sidled between the chairs to the aisle, where she turned and walked towards the back. She saw James looking at her and her heart jumped. She noticed his fine brown hair, gray eyes, and handsome face. He was looking directly at her, staring at her. She put her glasses back on. *Has he been watching me? Waiting for me?* She felt hunted and, in a way, James *was* hunting her. The thought made her uncomfortable. Her father's face floated in her mind, warning her about men, but then James smiled and her fear melted away.

He gestured, asking whether she would speak with him. She looked away shyly at first, but then nodded. As she approached him, he held out his hand. "James, James Brighton." He looked directly into her eyes, which blinked at him from behind glasses.

"I'm Anya." She blushed and then looked down at her shoes.

He asked with a warm, but impertinent tone, "So, do you have a last name?"

"Anya Andersen." She looked up into his face and offered her hand, which he took and held, feeling the warm delicacy of her fingers. She liked the touch of his hand and the look of his face. Her pupils dilated. His dilated in return.

He let go of her hand and cleared his throat. "So, what did you think of it? The reading? Did you like it?"

She nodded. "It was okay."

"Just okay?"

"Well, listening to the poet read his work is much better than reading poetry silently to yourself. I mean, poets know exactly how to read their poetry, where to inflect their voice, where to pause, what to emphasize. Reading a poem properly is like acting. David does that well, but I'm not that big a fan of his themes or metaphors and besides, nothing rhymes. I like rhyming poems like *Stopping by the Woods on a Snowy Evening*." She felt at ease and took off her glasses, but kept them in her hand.

"Who's David? Was this guy David?"

"David Meltzer, silly. Didn't you know? He's a beat poet. Do you like beat poetry?"

"Beat? Do you mean like, *'death and purgetoried our torsos, with drugs, with dreams, with waking nightmares,'* and the possibility of HIV infection?"

"Howl! But it doesn't mention HIV... You must like poetry."

"Not much, not really. I liked Howl, I guess, at some point in the past when I was in college. You sound like an expert."

"I know something about poetry. Did you like David?"

"Didn't hear a word; wasn't listening at all; don't know who he is. I'm not really into poetry, either."

She put her glasses back on, crossed her arms across her chest, and said, "I don't understand... then, why did you come if you don't like poetry?"

"Umm, well, I mean, I was in the neighborhood, and, uh, sort of bored, so I stopped in. What about you?"

"I'm a writer. Attending poetry readings is part of that. What do you do?"

"Ah, you're a writer. I am not a writer. I am not a poet. I am not a painter. I am not a musician. I am not a lawyer. I am not a doctor. I am not. I am not."

"Defining yourself by who you aren't doesn't make any sense."

"It does if the list is long enough. What do you write about?"

"Romance, mostly. Well, primarily."

"With white knights rescuing damsels from dragons?"

"More contemporary, but there are similarities."

"I'm intrigued. I want to hear more. May I buy you coffee?" he asked. She nodded. "Let's go." She followed him out of the bookstore into the cool evening air and bustling street.

Anya had limited experience with men. In fact, going to coffee with a stranger in the city was a new experience. Her overly protective father smothered her adolescence, arresting her social development. She had escaped the small agriculture town of Buelton, California at twenty after attending community college there. She transferred to San Francisco State, where she earned a BA in Creative Writing. She had graduated a year before.

"When did you start writing?" he asked.

"When I was a kid and was bored, I told myself stories. Then, I started writing them down because I liked re-reading them."

"Liked re-reading them?"

"That's why I wrote them down. At first, I told them to myself, and then one day I just started to write them down and re-write them, changing things around each time: the characters, their names, how they looked and spoke, their habits." She trailed off and became quiet.

"I've tried to write, but it turns into scribble," he said.

"Scribble? You mean with a pencil?"

"No, I scribble with MS Word."

But that's not possible, she thought, while absent mindedly saying, "I use MS Word, too."

"We use the same word processor! Doesn't that mean we were meant for each other?"

"Only geeks say things like that."

"Yow, that hurt. I am wounded!" he felt pinned and wriggling on the wall.

"Sorry. I hope it was only a flesh wound."

It was only a flesh wound. He picked himself up, brushed himself off, and bravely continued. "You know, because we use the same word processor, we can exchange files!"

"I don't know you well enough to exchange files."

"Why, what are you afraid of?"

"Viruses!"

"Nice… so, what would if find if I opened your files, Anya?"

"Well, um, unfinished stories… weird ideas … epiphanies… stuff like that."

"Epiphanies! I can't remember the last time I had an epiphany. I guess you have a diary full of them."

"No, not a diary. It's a collection of broken thoughts. I call them Shards, James."

"James!" he said. "You know, that is the first time you've said my name. I am deeply moved."

"You are so sarcastic." She leaned towards him playfully, coming close to his face, looking directly into his eyes, inhaling and then moving away.

They arrived at the café. He opened the door for her. Once inside, he signaled a waiter who led them to a table by the window.

"What have you published?" he asked.

"A few short stories in local newspapers, literature journals in college. Things like that."

"Local papers? Which ones?"

"The *Santa Ynez News* and the *Lompoc Record*."

"The *Lompoc Record*? What's that?" He looked incredulous.

"Lompoc is near my home town, Buelton. It's their newspaper."

"Where?"

"Buelton, near Solvang?"

"Oh, yeah, I've been to Solvang."

"I've written some novels. Well, the first two aren't any good, but I'm working on one that is going to be great."

"Do you make any money from it?"

"Practically nothing."

"Then why do it?"

"It is part of who I am. For money, I tutor English, reading, and writing. What about you? I know what you're not, but 'I know not what you are'."

"I'm a collector."

"Really? What do you collect?"

"Rare guitars," he said, cocked his head to one side, and raised an eyebrow as if he expected her to be impressed.

What a pretension, she thought, but politely said, "Gee, that sounds interesting."

"You have no idea. It is interesting. There's a lot to know, lots of details."

"So, what are some details about rare guitars?"

"Like one I bought a few months ago at an estate sale in Tahoe City, you know, near Lake Tahoe. A rich guy died and he had a lot of stuff. There was an auction. I drove up. Stayed in Squaw Valley, skied a few days then went to the auction. He had one guitar I wanted. It was a 1957 Les Paul Custom. It is sooooo coooool. Totally black. They call it 'Black Beauty'. It has a mahogany neck and an ebony fingerboard with inlaid mother of pearl fret markers that are white and shiny and contrast amazingly with the black. It's signed by Les Paul... Here are some pictures of it." He held up his cell phone.

"Did you buy it?"

"I stole it for three thousand dollars. I can get twenty thousand in Japan. I do about twenty deals a year. I always have a deal in the air, if you know what I mean. Would you like to come to an auction sometime? I do a lot of traveling because of it, across the US, England, Canada, Japan, Germany, France."

"Um… I don't know," she replied. An awkward silence followed.

James then tapped on the window and said, "See that bum out there? I spoke to him earlier tonight."

"About what? Did he tell you why he became a bum?"

"No, no, well, it's not as though we had a chat or anything like that. He just asked for food, sorry beggar that he is. After coffee, let's take him out to eat."

"Are you kidding?"

"Not at all. He's hungry. We can take him to a sandwich shop. Buy him dinner. A modest act of charity, wouldn't you say? You can ask him why he chose a beggar life-style."

"When you put it that way, all right."

After coffee, they walked outside to the sidewalk. James scanned the street for the bum. "I don't see him." He waited a few minutes and then said, "Well, it looks like he's gone. Listen, I have absolutely nothing to do tonight. Want to take a walk or something? Or we could share a dessert at the top of the Mark Hopkins."

"I'm afraid not, I have to get going. I'm tutoring in the morning."

"Oh, come on. I'm safe. I am so bored. Let's do something."

"I'm sorry."

"Listen, is there any way I could see you again? Maybe meet for dinner and a show? Something like that?" he asked.

"Yes, I think so," she said and waved down a cab.

"How do I get in touch with you?"

"Look me up on Facebook. Look for Anya Andersen, Author." A cab pulled up. She opened the door and got in. "Goodnight, James… It was a pleasure." And then she said to the driver, "Please, take me to 2501 Crestline Drive in Twin Peaks."

"Yes, Miss."

The cab pulled away from the curb, leaving James alone with the present tense and his ennui. He considered scuttling back into his shell, but then he spotted the bum. He decided to dine with the bum instead.

CHAPTER 4

As the cab pulled away, Anya twisted around to look back at James, who stood on the sidewalk. She made eye contact and smiled as the growing distance erased the details of his face. She felt warm and fuzzy, and nearly purred as she dipped her head to the right in repose, staring blankly into space.

She said aloud, "Who is this James character anyway?"

"Did you say something, Miss?" the driver asked.

"No, nothing. Not a thing."

She replayed the animation of his face in her mind: his smirking lips, undulating brows, and dilating pupils. He wore jeans and a tight-fitting blue shirt that outlined his fit, upper body. As she thought about him, a trickle of body chemistry reached a small crescendo and then faded away, leaving behind a mild afterglow. After a short pause, she thought about him again and achieved similar results.

Her phone pinged. It was a Facebook friend request from James. *That was fast.* His attention and interest fanned a faint flicker that tickled.

"Here we are. 2501 Twin Peaks," the driver announced.

She paid the cabby and walked towards the front door, behind which she heard a yapping dog tap dancing on the marble floor inside.

"It's your Mommy, Norman. I'm home," she cooed.

Norman, a golden Papillon, responded with an affectionate dog purr. Anya was not really his mommy. His real mommy was Roger. Roger was one of Anya's roommates. Roger and Frederick were a cute married couple in their late thirties. Roger was the mom and Frederick, although not exactly the dad, was the more powerful of the two and also the more successful, a Professor of Medicine at the University of San Francisco. Frederick paid for the house they co-owned. It was community property. Anya rented a room from them.

The home in Twin Peaks overlooked the Height District and Golden Gate Park. Years earlier, during her senior year at San Francisco State, she moved in with them. They had bonded into a close threesome, like a family. The men knew all of Anya's secrets. Roger was particularly mothering and possessive, constantly advising her.

Roger called out to her, bending her name from Anya into *Ownya*, an affectation that became his pet name for her. "Where have you been, Ownya?" he scolded.

She entered the living room and found the men sitting on the sofa watching *Project Runway*. She sat on a chair by the sofa. Norman hopped into her lap and lay down. She stroked his head with both hands and looked into his face. "You are such a good boy."

Roger had coiffed blond hair, which he wore differently each day. Today, he had bangs parted down the center, each hair perfectly placed. Frederick had salt and pepper hair, neatly cut. He was professional looking and slightly older.

"What have you been doing all this time? We expected you an hour ago," Roger said and muted the TV.

"Yes, and you missed dinner and most of episode seven," Frederick added with indignation. Cocktails, dinner, and *Project Runway* were a weekly ritual.

"I know. I should have called."

"Oh, my God, Anya! You missed Sandro's complete break down!" Roger went on. "He totally cracked up. He couldn't take the pressure." Sandro was a contestant on *Project Runway*.

"Too bad. I thought he was good. Really creative," Anya said.

"I didn't like him at all," Roger sniffed.

"He made a complete fool out of himself tonight," Frederick added.

"Yes, a complete idiot," Roger said.

"But it was noble of him to speak out in defense of Katisha," Frederick said.

"What did she make?" Anya asked.

Roger said, with mild distain, "Another pant suit. This is her third pant suit. It is so boring, and furthermore, it wasn't noble of Sandro at all to defend her. She's terrible!"

"When he realized he had blown it, he melted down with the cameras rolling," Frederick said.

"Oh, my God! Ownya, you should have seen it," Roger said, hands on cheeks.

"The panic in his face... They caught the whole thing and when they replayed it, he just died," Frederick said.

"So humiliating. Even I cringed! And I hate Sandro," Roger said.

"He stormed out of the studio and quit. Just like that!" Frederick added and snapped his fingers.

"No!" she said. "Do you think they'll eliminate someone else tonight, even though Sandro quit?"

"Oh, I'm sure they will. The Princess is so exacting," Frederick said.

"Yes, I agree, and it's so horrible and so stressful, I don't think I can watch it," Roger covered his eyes.

"It's back on," Frederick said and unmuted the television.

"They're going to replay part of it. Better buckle your seat belts, it's going to be a long episode," Roger said.

Together, they watched Sandro's meltdown. All three of them flinched at his psychic pain, even though Roger secretly relished his suffering. Then, as predicted, Katisha was eliminated. She broke down and cried.

Roger muted the TV and said with pride, "I told you she'd eliminate Katisha."

Frederick said, "So, tell us where you've been, Ownya."

"I met a man tonight."

Both of their heads turned toward her in unison.

"Oh, my God! Our little girl has met a man. I think I have a tear in my eye."

"Well, my dear Anya, it is about time," Frederick said.

Although Anya was twenty-three, she had had only one boyfriend. Her overly protective father had left her shy, bookish, and awkward.

"Tell us all about him, Ownya," Roger asked.

"His name is James."

"James what?" Frederick asked.

"Brighton."

"James Brighton. Sounds waspy. Tell us more."

"There's nothing much to say about him," she said and then blushed.

"Oh, look, Freddie. Ms. Ownya is blushing. I think there is much more to this man than just a name."

"Well, his business is rare guitars," she said.

"Rare guitars?" Frederick looked unimpressed.

"Yes, rare guitars. He buys and sells them."

"That sounds dubious," Frederick said.

"Yes, marginal, but romantic somehow," Roger sighed. "You didn't sleep with him already, did you?"

She threw a couch pillow at him.

"Okay, I was kidding. But did you kiss him?" Roger asked with a small voice.

"Of course not. I just met him. We're Facebook friends, though."

"So soon! That's life in the internet era, isn't it, Frederick."

"Here's his picture." She handed the men her phone.

"Oh, he's cute. Are you sure he's straight? Maybe I want to go out with him," Frederick joked.

"Oh, Freddie! You say such mean things to make me jealous," Roger said.

"Look, there's a message." Frederick handed the phone back to her.

She opened the message. "He wants to go out tomorrow, in the afternoon. He wants to meet at Golden Gate Park at around 2 pm. He says, 'Bring your writing'."

"Oh, the park," Roger said dreamily. "She has a date in the park with James, that handsome devil. How romantic." He let out a sigh and then said, "We did such naughty things in the park, didn't we, Frederick. Should we let her go all by herself?"

"I don't know. Anya, do you trust this man? This mysterious rare guitar dealer?" Frederick asked.

"It sounds dangerous. I mean, he picked her up off the street. Maybe we should chaperon," Roger said.

"That's ridiculous," she said.

"Where did you meet this rare guitar dealer, anyway?" Roger asked.

"City Lights. There was a poetry reading."

"He likes poetry. Well, that's a plus," Roger said.

"No, actually, he doesn't like poetry at all."

"Then, why was he there?" Roger asked.

"I think he's a spy," Frederick said.

"Yes, James Brighton Bond. He's trying to penetrate your secret, private life," Roger said.

"What does that even mean?" Anya said.

"We want to meet him," Roger said. "We can't just let you go out with a stranger to the park alone."

Frederick said, "I'm not going to be here in the afternoon. I have meetings all day."

"Oh, well," he sighed. "I guess it's left to me then. I will have to meet him."

"He wants to meet me in the park, though."

"No, I'm sorry. That is not acceptable. Ask him to pick you up here."

She did ask and James agreed.

CHAPTER 5

After Anya left James standing on the sidewalk, he saw the bum. He hustled him into a sandwich shop and bought him five foot-long subway sandwiches, ten bags of chips, twelve cookies, and an extra-large coke with no ice. His name was Chip. He grew up in a small town in Washington. His alcoholic father threw him out of the house at age sixteen. He had been homeless ever since.

As depressing as Chip was, James was in a great mood. Meeting Anya pulled him out of his months-long stupor. He felt rejuvenated, full of energy, almost enthusiastic. He decided to photograph the Black Beauty that night. He had possessed her for several months, and by now, knew well her curves, and every nook and cranny. He had played Brown Sugar on Black Beauty, coaxing from her fine, warm tones, deep purple in color and viscous, like liquid chocolate.

When Black Beauty was new, he obsessed over her and kept her near the chaise lounge so that he could turn his head and see her whenever he wanted, or reach out and touch her, or hold her in his arms and fawn over her, teasing out her secrets. Over the weeks, he thought of Black Beauty often. She came to mind during idle moments or appeared in dreams, surreal and exaggerated. Finally, a complete picture of her emerged and it was time to photograph.

As soon as he arrived home after dining with Chip, he dashed to the living room, grabbed Black Beauty, and zipped upstairs to the photography studio. The studio had been the master bedroom before James converted it. It was large, eight hundred square feet. He kept photographic equipment in the walk-in closet. He had covered the windows with black curtains to keep out the light. There was a huge, wall-sized picture of a guitar called the 'Lake Placid Blue', a 1954 Fender Stratocaster. As the name suggested, it was pale blue. He made the image from smaller pictures of it that he printed and fit together, like puzzle pieces, all close ups of details, like the headstock, fret markers, and the serial number, which was stamped on a small metal plate.

He pulled a large c-stand from the closet, positioned it in front of a blue backdrop and slid the Black Beauty into the saddle of the c-stand. Except for a thin, white strip that encircles her perimeter and the white mother-of-pearl fret markers, the Black Beauty was totally jet black; black body, fingerboard, pick guard, and dials.

He wanted to hear music while he worked, so he turned on an old stereo that his parents bought in the 1980s. It was a bit of an antique. It had a turntable, amplifier, and a carousel CD player that held nearly two hundred CDs. He pressed buttons and turned knobs until the carousel whirred to life. It randomly selected a CD, which began to play Bach's "Air on a G-String". The methodical procession of notes formed long, unbroken musical thoughts, and stirred in him a reverie that guided him as he worked. He placed another c-stand in front of the guitar, fastened a camera to it and then took a volley of shots. He repositioned the camera and took more. He continued like this, moving the guitar and camera into different positions while changing lenses, filters, and lights, taking more photos with each configuration. He continued until he was sick of it. Then he stopped.

***

The next day, in the late morning, just up the hill from James' home in the Marina, Anya rang the doorbell of a stately San Franciscan home in Pacific Heights on Broadway Avenue. The house was made of brick. The front door and windows were framed in white concrete entablature and pediment. The roof was steep and made of gray slate from which protruded three dormer windows that ran the length of the third floor. A low parapet of white balustrades separated a small courtyard in front of the house from the sidewalk.

She was there to tutor François Templar in English. He was a pimpled thirteen-year-old who had been flunking English at the local boy's school, to the extreme shame to his parents. François was the unwanted child from a second marriage and his father was contemptuous of him. His mother was in her mid-forties. His father was over sixty. His father had left his first wife and disowned his previous children, out of lust for another woman, Nora. Nora had been pretty, but was now obese. She had married him for his money. Now, he had an extra child and was trapped. He hated his situation and verbally abused François regularly, as a way to scratch the nagging itch of his unhappiness.

François answered the door and was thrilled to see Anya. She was one of the few supportive adults in his life and he had a crush on her. He glowed with romantic feelings, wagging with joy, like a puppy. His crush inspired him. His grades improved and an appreciation of literature took hold.

"Hello, Mr. Temblor. How are you today?" she said and gave him a hug.

"I am so glad you're here. I worked on the Poem. I want to show you!" His assignment was to analyze selected lines of the poem, *Ode on a Grecian Urn*. He led her to the dining room, where she took her place at the head of the table. He sat by her amid papers and pens, books and a laptop, which displayed several lines of the poem.

"Here," he slid the laptop over to her and gave her a moment to focus. Then he quoted, "'Heard melodies are sweet, but those unheard, Are sweeter;'"

"Very good, François. What do you think of this line?"

"Well, music doesn't have a taste, so, music being sweet seems impossible."

"Well, first of all, 'sweet' is a metaphor. It is not meant to be taken literally. And by the way, there are people who see colors when they hear music. They have a condition called Synesthesia, so the idea of music having a taste is not that farfetched."

"What is Sin-o-stesia?"

"Synesthesia. Some people perceive things through more than one sense. So, if I play a middle-C on the piano, they will see a color, like blue. D might be another color, say green."

"Wow! I wonder which note for purple is." He stared off into space, pondering Synesthesia while wiggling his legs with nervous energy.

"What else? How about the first line of the poem?" she asked.

"Oh, you mean, 'Thou still unravish'd bride of quietness'. Well, first of all, unravish'd is misspelled. See?" He pointed to the laptop screen.

"That's because he's taking poetic license. You know what he means even if it is misspelled."

"Okay. Then there's this: if she's unravished, it means she's a virgin. She hasn't had sex before."

"Yes, well, that's another metaphor. She is the bride of 'quietness'. Not a real person."

"Have you ever had sex before, Anya?"

"François! I am shocked at such a question. It just isn't appropriate."

"I know." He laid his head down on the table, despairing and embarrassed. "I can't help it. I hope you haven't. I hope you are a virgin. I hope you are unravished," he moaned, and then looked at her with horror over what he had just confessed. He hid his face in his hands.

She smirked at him. "And why does that matter to you?"

"I would be jealous."

"It is none of your business," she said, breaking his heart just a little bit.

CHAPTER 6

Later that day, after Anya's lesson with François, James pulled up in front of Anya's place on Crestline Drive in Twin Peaks. He sent a text message to her announcing his arrival. Her phone pinged and she read the message. "Oh, he's here. I'll go get him."

"You'll do no such thing, Ownya," Roger said. "You must make him wait, just a little bit. Text him back this, 'Hi James, I'm not ready. Please, ring the bell. My roommate will let you in'."

"I don't think that's very polite."

"It's perfectly fine to make the man wait. I did it all the time. And besides, you're not going out with this completely strange man until I'm sure he's not a deranged psychopath."

She took his advice and typed into her phone. "Text sent."

"Now, go upstairs to your room."

"What?"

"Shoo. Out." He gestured. "I'll call you when it's time."

Anya left the living room. The doorbell rang and Roger shuffled through the living room towards the stairs. He paused in front of a mirror and touched the sides of his head, fixing stray hairs, before skipping down the stairs to the door. He opened it. "You must be James. I'm

Roger. Soooo nice to meet you."

James blinked at Roger's Mikado-yellow pants and tiffany-blue, slim-fit shirt. His blemish-free face shined as though he wore creams to bed each night. His brows looked plucked and trimmed. His coiffed hair rose over his forehead like a blond wave about to break.

James cautiously said, "Nice to meet you."

James wore blue Levis, hiking boots, and a red long sleeve tee shirt that said 'Cabo San Lucas' on the front. He carried an SLR camera with a long telephoto lens in his hand.

Roger's eyes and lips formed Os as he looked James up and down, panning from his face to his hips and then back again. *My, my. He's much better looking in the flesh. So 'Men-at-Work'*, he thought. He wiggled just a teeny bit while saying, "Ownya is nearly ready."

"Ownya? Do you mean Anya?"

"Yes, of course, Anya. I say it with a long O, 'Ownya'. It's my special name for her." Roger tipped his head from side to side, as he spoke.

"Right."

"Well, never mind. Would you be kind enough to come inside and wait?"

"Okay." James shrugged.

"Follow me." Roger turned and hopped up the stairs like a rabbit. James ambled after him. At the top of the stairs stood a five-foot-tall plaster of Paris statue of Michelangelo's David that wore Groucho Marx glasses and a mustache like a fig leaf over the statue's genitals, making a nose with its penis. The décor of their home was baroque, garish, and bawdy with pinks, lavenders, and reds. Norman's nails clicked on the white marble floor as he trotted over to James and sniffed his leg and then licked it, leaving a wet spot on his pants. James grimaced.

James recognized a reproduction of Charles Demuth's *Turkish Bath* hanging in the living room and felt mildly repulsed by the chest hair and genitals of naked men. A five hundred line Persian rug, swirling with Islamic geometry, covered the floor in the center of the room. A sectioned white sofa with three sides circumscribed the rug and faced the fireplace, to the left of which was a television. Most of the sofa pillows were shaped like hearts and lips, but one was a purple penis.

"Please, sit," Roger gestured towards the couch.

James sat amid the hearts, far away from the rude penis.

"Tea? Water?"

"Water, thanks."

"James is here, dear," Roger called to Anya as he walked to the kitchen to get water, hips wiggling.

"Thanks, Roger. I'll be down in a minute."

James was not homophobic at all. He had friends who were gay and had learned how to deal with them, which was mostly to treat them like other men. Still, even with the absence of homophobia, James found depictions of men's bodies and genitals gross. He did not know why, he just did. *And there's nothing wrong with that,* he reassured himself.

Roger returned with water, placed it on the coffee table by the sofa, sat down, and said, "So, Ownya tells me you have a rare guitar business or something silly like that. Is that true?" He looked at James and batted his eyes.

"Yeah."

"Is that a good business to be in?" Knowing he had asked a delicate question, Roger glanced away momentarily, as if to give James privacy while he reacted to the question.

"It depends on whether you like guitars, I guess," James said stoically.

"Do you play?"

"Yeah, a little."

"But not really?"

"I had a band in high school. We sucked. We had a good name, though."

"A good name?"

"Roxx, spelled like this: R-O-X-X."

"That is a good name, but the band, as you say, sucked?"

"Right."

"So, you just like to look at guitars or something like that?"

"I play a little, but mostly I trade them and make money."

"Do you mind if I ask how much a business like that makes?"

"Yes."

"Yes, what?"

"I do mind you asking how much."

"Oh dear, have I hit a nerve? I have, haven't I? I am so sorry." Roger raised a hand to his cheek, and shifted his body into his 'Oh, My God!' posture.

"I have plenty of money," James said.

"And where did you say you lived?"

"I didn't say."

"I am sorry about all the questions, but we worry about our little Ownya."

"Why is that?"

"Well, we just want to be sure she doesn't get involved with any undesirable characters."

"I thought you are her roommate, not her mom," James said.

Just then, Anya appeared and paused at the entrance of the living room. The men stopped talking and turned towards her in slow motion. James' eyes sought Anya's, which bashfully darted away, but then returned to him with a radiant gaze that made his heart leap. He rose from the sofa and crossed the room in silence to greet her, taking her hand. They stood in quiet communion.

"Oh, my … I think I hear violins playing," Roger said with romantic sincerity. The two were so entranced they did not hear him at all. "Ah-hem," Roger cleared his voice. "I'm still here people!" They turned and looked at him. "What exactly are you two planning to do today?"

"We're going to the park, hit the De Young, walk in the gardens, stuff like that," James said.

"That sounds very nice, very nice indeed. Perhaps, a bit too nice. All right, you are now free to go. Now, you take care of our Ownya, James."

James felt like saying, 'Yes, Ma'am', but instead, shrugged and said, "Of course."

"And Ownya, as tempted as you might be, don't do anything with James I wouldn't do. Just a warning."

"Astonishing," James mumbled to himself. It was a critical comment, but James also liked this warm, concerned, effeminate man.

They followed Roger down the stairs. He opened the door to the street. "It looks like fog is already rolling in quietly, 'on little cat's feet' as they say. Ownya, did you take a jacket?"

"I have long sleeves."

They crossed the street to his car. James held the door for Anya as she climbed into his car and then closed it. He rounded the car to the driver's seat and got in. After carefully backing out onto the street, they pulled away while Roger watched, arms folded as if mildly dismayed.

CHAPTER 7

"So, at last we're alone. I didn't expect to find you living with two men. I met Roger. What's the other one like?" James asked.

"Frederick. He's a doctor. He wasn't home."

"Should I be jealous?"

"Jealous? You and I don't know each other well enough for that. Besides, they're married."

"Are their spouses living there, too?"

"No, no, no. They're married to each other."

"Ooooooooh! I guess I should've seen that coming. So, you're living with two married men. That's sort of 'Radical Chic', isn't it?"

"I guess," she replied and changed the subject. "I noticed you brought a camera." She impulsively reached for the long telephoto lens lying between his legs, violating his personal space. As her fingers curled around it, contracting muscles undulated across his gut, like ripples on a pond. He gasped. She noticed the surprise in his face and let go of it. He relaxed.

"Yeah, I like to take photos. It's how I express my inner-self."

"But I thought you said you are the 'Man who is not'?" she joked.

"Okay, I admit it. I don't really have an inner-self."

"Of course, you do. I am looking forward to meeting him, someday."

"The reason I do the photos is because I like to look at them later. A past moment brought back to the present. You know what I mean?" He changed the subject. "So, where do you want to go in the park?"

"I don't know. Where do you want to go?"

"Is the art museum okay?" he asked and she nodded.

James parked on John F. Kennedy Drive. They left the car and walked the quarter mile or so to the De Young which is on the north side of the Music Concourse.

"So, do you have a lot of tutoring gigs?"

"I have enough. This one is with a very pouty, spoiled boy. His family has been in San Francisco since the 1860s, five generations, the 'Temblars'. They're a very proud family. The boy's name is François. He's thirteen. He goes to a private school called Town School. He's failing English, History, Math… just about everything. I'm just one of several tutors trying to 'rescue him'. At least, that's the way his father puts it. I have others, another six or so one-on-one engagements. I see them several times a week. I teach them mostly the mechanics of writing; grammar, spelling, expository essay structure, things like that. I teach Shakespeare to one of them. I'm analyzing a classic poem with François. I also have an ESL class, around ten students."

"Sounds like you're busy."

They arrived at the concourse near the De Young and she noticed the Academy of Sciences across the concourse. "Have you been to the Science Museum?" she asked.

"Yeah. Many times, but it's been years," he said, nodding his head.

"We should go sometime."

"Sure."

James pointed at the De Young. "The De Young is just plain ugly. It looks like an air traffic control tower. Someday, it will turn green when the copper oxidizes. Then it will be *really ugly*!"

"I like it. Morphing into green is a metaphor, the color of life."

"Yeah, I guess. I still think it's ugly."

They stopped outside. "Okay, let's see, what they have today? Chinese Contemporary Art. Are you up for a little Chinese art?"

She shrugged indifferently.

"I'm not into it either," he said.

"How about the gift shop?"

"Sounds good."

They entered the shop. Anya browsed the kitschy memorabilia while James thumbed through a bin of posters. After a couple of minutes, she waved her hand in the air, dismissing all of it. "It's all chachka," she said, using a Yiddish word she had learned after moving to the city; a word not known in Buelton, her hometown. She joined James at the bin of posters and began looking through them.

"Look at this one," he held up a watercolor of a blue pond, orange carp, and green lily pads.

She liked it and joined him at an adjacent poster bin, fingering through posters until she came to one of an airline advertisement from the 1940s, Art Deco style. It read 'Imperial Airlines'. She held it up. "Look at this airline advertisement. Ever hear of Imperial Airlines?" James shook his head no. She continued, "1940. That was eighty years ago. I'm sure it went out of business a long time ago, lost, forgotten, never heard of again. All that remains is a poster."

"Hey, look at this," He held up an Erte painting of a Ballerina in red and gold. "It was a *Harper's Bazaar* magazine cover from the 1920s. What do you think of it?"

"Beautiful."

"You know, you can buy these as numbered lithographs. I think people consider them art, but there are thousands of them. They're like expensive posters."

"You really are a snob, James."

"So?"

"I don't like that about you."

"Uh, sorry."

She came across a poster that startled her and she froze. It was *In Front of the Mirror* by the Swedish artist, Carl Larsson. She put on her glasses so she could inspect it in detail. The picture showed a large mirror, which covered a wall floor to ceiling, in a private study or library, which was probably part of a much larger home or mansion. The mirror was framed by golden Babylonian iconography. Perched on top of the mirror, on the left and right, were two winged beasts with the bodies of lions and the heads of women.

The painting displayed the profile of a young nude woman in a classical pose with a crescent of leaves in her hair. The mirror reflected her backside, which made both her front and backside visible. Also, in the mirror was the startling reflection of a man who, at first, seemed to be leering at her. He wore formal dress, for a night on the town, of striped slacks, a white silk shirt, and an unbuttoned vest. A watch chain dangled from the vest and disappeared into his pants pocket. He held a paintbrush and stood by an easel. She stood nude before him. He was painting her.

As Anya looked at the poster, her feelings about it changed. His leer became serious concentration and from there it morphed into frustration, as if he was unable to express the beauty he perceived. He looked helpless in the face of it, weak, almost comical. Although he was part of the painting, he was also an outsider, separate from her, powerful and severe in his civilized dress compared to her natural, unprotected beauty. His stubble and grit abraded the scene and contrasted with her soft, smooth skin. He commanded over her, forming her onto the canvas, looking hungry with desire, but impotent because what he wanted was beyond his reach.

The model's head hung slightly as though she was fatigued. Anya wondered how many times the woman had posed for the artist. She imagined the artist sought something in the model that he could not define and would never know, but was convinced was there. Most of all, the woman seemed vulnerable and exposed. A ball of anxiety congealed in Anya's belly.

"What do you think of it?" James broke the silence.

She shuddered and said, "I don't like it at all. It makes me uncomfortable."

"Why?" he asked.

"I can't say, exactly."

"It captures a moment between them. No? A very personal, private moment, wouldn't you say?"

"It makes me feel very uncomfortable." Anya said.

"Why?"

"She just seems so naked."

"Well, she is nude, isn't she? I mean, that's the main point of the picture, isn't it?"

"Yes, but she seems so … um … extra naked."

"What? 'Extra naked'. What does that mean?"

"I don't know how else to say it. I guess it's because he's clothed and so focused on her, like she's under a microscope. It magnifies her nakedness, her vulnerability."

"I think it magnifies her beauty. I like it. I think it's sexy."

"Well, to each his own," she said. "What would possess a woman to do something like this? For money? I think she was poor. It's like prostitution or pornography."

"I really disagree. Porn is cheap, mass-produced. This is art. It requires years of patience, experience, inspiration."

"She's objectified by it."

"I disagree with that, too. They did this together, for art and probably also for love. It's not as though he carried her off and forced her to pose for him. This isn't against her will."

"She was coerced."

"Well, perhaps she was led, but that isn't coercion. It's collaboration. This is theirs, and with it, they achieved a sort of immortality. Look, here they are one hundred years later. The picture lives on."

"She seems so completely naked, so vulnerable and fragile, it gives me butterflies. Perhaps, it's the mirror that exposes her from all angles or the look on his face. Together, they strip her of any shred of ..." she trailed off, not able to find the exact words.

"Any shred of what, dignity? Are you saying she looks undignified? I think she's beautiful, and so does the painter. He is worshipping her. Venerating her."

"She is the object of his desire."

"She is the object of his love. This picture is about both of them and what they feel about each other. You know, this could be his wife or his lover. Love and desire drove them to this. He wanted to capture it, to take her into himself, and then pour her out onto canvas."

"You're daft."

"No, really. It is about love and art. Here, look at this." He pulled a poster of Botticelli's *Birth of Venus*. "You've seen this before?"

"Of course, I have. Everyone has."

"It's a classic, right? But it's a nude, isn't it? Is it pornographic?"

"Well, not exactly. I know it's supposed to be all about beauty and love, but that's all BS. It's really about something else."

"No, it really represents ethereal love, courtly love, sensuous beauty."

"I don't see how."

"Do you know how this was inspired?"

"What do you mean?"

"I mean, what inspired Botticelli to paint the *Birth of Venus.*"

"I have no idea."

"Well, there is a story about this renaissance lady who was in the Medici Court in the 1470s in Florence who was a great beauty. Her name was Simonetta something or other. She married an aristocrat. Anyway, a member of the Medici family expressed his 'Courtly Love' for her by entering a jousting tournament in her honor. He carried a banner with her image on it throughout the tournament. He was obsessed with her and made his obsession known publicly, but it was courtly love only. It made her famous. She became sort of like a beauty queen. Tragically, she died a year later."

"Oh, no! What did she die of?"

"Tuberculosis. She was only twenty-two. They buried her in a church in Florence. Years later, Botticelli, the painter, requested to be buried at the foot of her grave when he died, because he was still obsessed with her. His request was granted and that is where he is buried."

"So, she was the model for the painting then?"

"No, no, not at all. She couldn't have been the model. The *Birth of Venus* was painted eight years after she died. Also, she was a noble woman. She never would have posed nude. Botticelli would never have known her this way. But some people believe that she inspired it. So, that is an example of what I mean. Ethereal, courtly love."

"'My Courtney Love of courtly love' — I like the way that sounds," she said and made a mental note. Then she said, "I think the myth of the *Birth of Venus* isn't very ethereal at all. It's a very graphic, very dirty story. You might even think of it as porn. I'm not sure I feel comfortable telling you about it it's so vulgar."

"I love vulgarity. I consider vulgarity a fine art. You think the *Birth of Venus* is vulgar?" he said, referring to the painting. "I don't even think of it as a nude."

"Do you know the myth, the *Birth of Venus*?"

"Sure. She rose out of the sea and then she was born. So what?"

"There's a lot more to it than that."

"Like what?"

She stepped towards him, her face coming close to his as she said with a hushed voice, as if telling a secret, "It is all about insatiable desire." Then she paused, as if what she had said embarrassed her and she needed to regain her composure. "It's about Gaea, the earth goddess and Uranus, the sky god, and how he wouldn't stop, uh," she paused again, and then said, "screwing her."

"Come again?"

49

She blushed and came closer to him so he could better hear her while he inhaled the mist of her breath as she whispered. "He wouldn't stop screwing her."

"Oh… I get you now. 'Wouldn't stop screwing her'. Very interesting, please go on."

"So, he wouldn't stop… until someone cut off his genitals."

"Jezzus! Yowzer!" James flinched and yowled, startling the other shoppers, who all turned and looked. He glanced at the others and said meekly, "Sorry."

She cautiously continued, "They threw them into the ocean, his genitals, that is. They made foam in the sea, you know, like the foam that washes up on beaches. The foam fertilized the sea goddess."

"That's disgusting! I swear I'm never going in the ocean again!"

"This is how Venus was conceived, and when she was born she rose out of the sea. And because it was her 'birthday', she had no clothing on. The Sumerian version is even more gross."

"The Sumerian version? I'm not sure I want to know."

"Yes, you do. In their version, the sky god wouldn't stop until someone bit off his genitals."

"Bit… off… his genitals! Oh. My. God! I can't believe you just said that."

"I'm not making this up."

"You make it sound like it's all about unquenchable lust, but Venus also inspires an intellectual appreciation of beauty and courtly love and so on."

She gave him a skeptical look.

James then said, "The model for the painting wasn't Simonetta. Who do you think the real model was?"

"Who was it then?"

"No one knows."

"No one knows? You mean, her body has been seen by millions, but no one knows who she was? There's something obscene in that," she said.

"I'll bet it was better off that way. In those days, she would have been punished, followed through the streets, ridiculed, taunted, stoned."

"What year was this?" she asked.

"1480's," he said.

"She probably thought she was going to hell."

"Unless she confessed."

"She must have been a low woman, a whore, desperate, needing money," she said.

"Maybe. No one knows. All you can say for sure is that she was someone's child and that she lived to at least young adulthood. She might have been a whore. She might have been a sibling, someone's wife, someone's mother, someone's lover."

"In those days, posing nude would have meant eternal damnation."

"Yeah, an afterlife in a Hieronymus Bosch painting," James said. "What do you think of Hieronymus Bosch?"

"I don't know who he is."

"Here, just a second." He thumbed through the posters. "Ah ha, here's a Bosch. This one is called *Hell*."

"Horrible."

"Do you think the model for Botticelli's *Venus* ended up here in her afterlife?"

"No. She ended up with Botticelli, eternally being born. What do you think of Botticelli, that he would paint a nude like this?" she asked.

James shrugged.

"I hope they are both suffering in Hieronymus Bosch paintings," she said.

They walked out of the shop into the gray light of a foggy day. She said, "I know where we should go next: The Labyrinth. It's just across Martin Luther King Drive."

"Labyrinth? Like a maze or something?"

"Well, it reminds me of a labyrinth. That's what I call it. It's a tangle of trails and paths in the woods. You can get lost in it."

She took his hand and led him from the gift shop, past the Tea Garden, across Martin Luther King Drive, and into Anya's labyrinth.

"Do you think we'll see a Minotaur?" she asked.

"I hope so. I can photograph it." He then said, "You know, I really like your red hair. Do you know the first historical reference of red hair?"

"No."

"Herodotus, the Greek Historian, in his book, the first history book, he refers to these people who lived in what is now Ukraine. They were different from all other people because they had red hair and blue eyes."

"You're kidding."

"Nope."

After reaching the Labyrinth, they hiked in circles, trying to get lost but failed. Eventually, they decided to sit on a bench beside a path in the forest. The damp forest leaves dripped with condensed fog.

"Why don't you read me some of your writing?"

"I only brought one thing to read: a poem. Well, not really a poem, more of a rhyme than a poem." She shuffled through her pockets and pulled out a crumpled paper from one pocket and her glasses from another. "Here it is. It's called *Now!*" She read it aloud.

"Now!

A whisper mumbling through the leaves,
and warbling hum of birds and bees,
together with a tumbling breeze;
The Present humbly on her knees.

Every grain of time and space,
Slides by with momentary grace.
It would be to my disgrace,
To lose a second in my haste.

Persistent Memory helps us grasp,
Our Remembrance of Things Past,
Until the final breath or gasp,
The meaning of each moment's last.

The ever-present tense ticks by,
And bravely heaves a final sigh.
I hold my moments till they die,
Like this one, shall we say goodbye?"

She stopped and looked up into the trees.

"Very Good. Really, really good," he gushed. "Did you really write that? I want to photograph you, right now, just as you are, lost in the Labyrinth." He stepped away, pointed his camera and snapped and then snapped again. "Now, I want you to read the poem. I want to photograph you while you read." She read it again while his camera snapped away.

Later that afternoon, after dropping Anya off at her place in Twin Peaks, his constant companion, ennui, engulfed him in the gray monotony of the present tense. He had nothing to do, nowhere to go, nothing to think.

Without a thought, am I not?

He decided to drown his ennui in sake and yakitori at Mokutanya, a quiet kushiyaki place in Japan Town. It served barbecued skewers of Kobe Beef from Japan, as well as skewers of Kobe Beef from the USA, which tasted nothing like the other, and skewers of chicken thigh meat and wing meat, which have minutely different flavors undetectable by Americans, but distinguished by the Japanese, and then there were the strange skewers of chicken skin, cartilage, and hearts — three of James' favorites. He kept a bottle of Saki at the restaurant, like one might keep bottles of booze at a golf club. The waitresses were all young, pretty, and Asian, except for one voluptuous African American woman who James thought was beautiful. All were polite, talkative, and fraternized with the customers.

To get to Mokutanya, he drove up Webster from Market to Post, passing beneath the pedestrian bridge that connected the malls on either side of Webster in J-Town. He parked and found his way through the mall to the restaurant. While they prepared his table, he waited in the lobby of Mokutanya by a waterfall that trickled into a Koi pond with lily pads and mottled fish, orange, white, and black.

His reflection floated in the pond, rippling when Koi broke the surface. Phantasmagoria magnified his reflection and the sound of the trickling water. His peripheral vision darkened, leaving him alone with his face reflected in the Koi pond. Time slowed while dread began to twist in his stomach. To distract himself, he brought his camera up to his eye and pointed it at the reflection, which had now changed into an image of him holding a camera. He withdrew the camera and his reflection returned. Then, in his mind's eye, a mental image of Anya replaced his reflection, and he began to think of her instead of himself. He reviewed the shots he had taken that day, all of her. "Anya makes me happy," he said out load.

He texted her, 'What shall we do tomorrow?' and then sat quietly and waited for a reply.

Anya arrived home, stopped at the front door, and held on to her lingering feelings for a moment, until Norman, Roger's Papillon, began barking.

Roger called out, "Ownya is that you?"

"Yes."

"Well, come upstairs and tell me all about your date."

They sat in the living room while she told him about the trip to the park, the posters, and their conversation about the myth of Venus and the sky god whose genitals had been cut off.

"Oh dear, you told him that? That's pretty naughty. I hope he doesn't think you're some sort of pervert," Roger said, and then added, "I'm sure he doesn't."

"He doesn't," she confirmed and then continued about the Labyrinth, the poem, and the camera.

"Yes, I notice that big, dangling telephoto lens," he said while wiggling his eyebrows. "You say he uses it to express his 'inner-self'.

I'm not sure how I feel about that. And he's a guitar dealer. He seems like a dubious person to me."

The tedious debriefing ended and she went to her room, opened her iMac, and waited while her mind descended into herself. She reviewed the day, recalling Golden Gate Park, the Labyrinth, reading her poem, the photographs, the cool fog, eucalyptus trees, and questions about *The Birth of Venus*, as well as the woman who posed for it. 'My Courtney Love of courtly love', kept repeating in her mind.

She said aloud to herself, "'My Courtney Love of courtly love … 'My Courtney Love of courtly love'" All of a sudden, quatrains appeared in her mind, rhythmic and rhyming, preassembled, appearing without conscious thought like a minor miracle. She quickly typed out the words before they faded.

My Courtney Love of Courtly Love
You are an Angel up above,
And always whom I'm thinking of
My Courtney Love of Courtly Love

You are the mistress of my muse
A delicious morsel that I choose
Nirvana when our gazes fuse
And when you're gone, I feel the blues

Ecstasy's too quickly spent
You left your flavor and your scent
To me what is to be is meant,
My Courtney Love, you're heaven sent

Then her phone pinged. There was a message from James. 'What shall we do tomorrow?'

CHAPTER 8

Now, months after their date in the park, they found themselves here, outside Feo's studio in a barrio, enveloped in damp fog and shivering, not because it was cold, but because of the humiliation they suffered from Feo's touching of Anya. As they waited for Uber to take them home, the session with Feo came back to Anya. She again felt his rough hands on her body. The feeling was subtle, but it bothered her and whenever she noticed it, she shifted her position until it left, but then it would return and each time it did, she shifted again. It was mild torment. James was calmer now, but still stewed in his jealousy. Neither of them had anticipated how painful the meeting would be.

A black Nissan Leaf arrived. "Here's our ride. A Leaf! Totally electric." He held open the door for her. She jumped in. He followed. She sidled over to him.

"What about food? Hungry?" he asked. He moved his lips to her forehead and said, "Let's go to La Mar in the Embarcadero near Market.
"

"I've never been there before. It sounds like Seafood."

"Peruvian sea food. La Mar *es una Cebicheria Peruana.*"

"What?"

"*Una Cebicheria.*"

"Whatever that is."

"You'll like it."

He opened his phone and began to type. "Okay. I just made a reservation in two hours. How about if Jack Hooker joins us?"

Jack was James' best friend. She had heard about him, but never met him. "Yes. I would like to meet him, finally." She fell back into his arms and laid her head on his shoulder. Soon, they arrived in the Marina. The Uber stopped in front of his house and they left the Leaf. He pressed numbers on a panel by the garage door and it opened.

His home was on Scott Street, between Chestnut and the Marina, a few blocks from the Palace of Fine Arts. His family had owned it for decades and it was now his. It was average for this area, about thirty-five hundred square feet. It had three bedrooms, three baths, a living room, dining room, kitchen, loft, an attic, and his studio. The house was painted sky blue and trimmed with fancy white molding, which together reminded him of Wedgewood porcelain. There were two rows of French windows on the first and second floors with red tile awnings. There was a single window for the attic on the third floor.

They hung their jackets in the garage, hurried upstairs to the kitchen, and walked to the living room, which overlooked the street through French windows. The living room had arched ceilings, a style popular in the 1930s when the house was built. The polished hardwood floors shined, reflecting the life of the household back onto itself.

They went to the living room where Anya flopped down on the chaise lounge. The chaise lounge was an unusual piece of furniture. It was larger than a king-size bed and covered by sepia-colored fleece; soft and warm. It stood on a huge Persian rug and was elevated by four scrolled-feet carved from mahogany. It faced the fireplace. He knelt by the fireplace, stacked logs inside and then lit the propane burners, whose blue flames blew fire on the wood until it burned. The fire's warmth filled the room.

The chaise lounge had a litter of pillows, all different shapes and colors. They used them to prop themselves up into various positions, especially to watch the TV, which was just to the right of the fireplace. There were a couple of neatly folded comforters they slept under and sometimes cuddled beneath on cold afternoons when it rained outside. It was their love nest.

She sat on the chaise lounge with the TV control in her hand, pressing buttons until a sound tract of rainfall, gentle thunder, and chirping birds began to play.

He disappeared into the kitchen. "Wine?" he called to her.

"Viognier, please" Viognier was her favorite. She loved its golden hue and tart finish of apricot. "Just a half glass, please."

"Yes, Madam." He returned to the room. "Here you are." He bowed, handed her the glass, and joined her on the chaise lounge.

"Thank you," she said. He slid over to her and folded his body until it matched the contour of hers, fitting into it like a puzzle piece. "Nothing for you?" she asked.

"No, thanks." He abstained because even a small amount of alcohol dulled his senses and he wanted them to be as acute as possible just now. She found a half glass just perfect, enough to relax her and erase inhibitions. She sipped and stared into the fire as the orange flames infused her face with the colors of dawn. The wine made her silly and her feelings of dread over the visit with Feo turned to mirth. She chuckled to herself.

"What's so funny?" he asked.

"This is such a naughty thing you want me to do next. It is sooooo naughty!"

"Well, it's not as though we haven't been naughty before."

She swatted his shoulder. "You make me feel like such a bad girl when you talk like that."

He rolled towards her until his torso was on hers. He brought his face up to hers and whispered, "Don't you like being my bad girl?" He dragged his lips across her cheek, to her ear, where he whispered, "I thought you liked it." Then he nipped at her ear.

"But this new thing with Feo, this is a little bit more..." she trailed off.

"A little bit more, what?"

"It's a little bit more bad."

"Come again? A little bit more bad? You're kidding me. More bad, than what?"

"Than the other bad things." She rocked her head coquettishly. "You know." She pouted at him.

What she said had both truths and falsehoods to it. The first falsehood was suggesting that he knew exactly what she meant by 'other bad things'. He did not know because they had done so many 'other bad things'. The next falsehood was calling them bad things because they were not really bad things at all, in the sense that they were not habit forming or self-destructive or even morally questionable as their entire love was well within the parameters of what is normal. The final falseness was referring to them as bad things because they both loved them so much that they were really 'good things'.

It was true that he was the one who choreographed these 'bad things', but he did it with such warmth that she felt safe, invited, and enticed by the promise of new intimacy. For her, each journey followed a similar course, starting with disbelief that he would propose such a queer thing. This was always followed by shock when she realized he meant it. However, in the end, she would always relent and accept it. From there, it became a gradual shedding of inhibitions, strand by strand, until everything was exposed and laid bare, after which she would become a willing participant exploring every detail of it.

For James, it was different. To him, each episode was an attempt to capture the illusive kernel of their love so that he could grasp it, then embed it in his mind, and be able to recall it whenever he wanted. It was his life, his work, his pleasure.

"'More bad' sounds ridiculous," James said. "How's about something a little more sophisticated?"

"Okay, how about perverted?" she laughed.

"Perverted? That's not very nice."

"I mean, what's wrong with you that you came up with this craziness?"

"I am deeply wounded." And he was.

"I'm sorry, James. I'm only teasing."

"Then you'll still do it?"

"Of course."

A moment of silence followed that was finally broken by James, who admitted the weirdness of it all. "Okay, so it is a bit ritualistic, isn't it?"

"Well, yes, it is, James. Maybe just a little bit."

"Well, more than a little. Maybe a lot," he chuckled.

"Oh, I'd say it's a lot. Most people would say, a lot. It's beyond ritualistic."

"What is beyond ritualistic?"

"What's beyond it? Enslavement to love," she said with a deadpan face.

"Does this make us 'love slaves?'"

"That sounds so dirty!" she squealed with laughter. Her silliness infected him and he chortled loudly. Soon, they lost all self-control and could not control their hysteria for at least a few minutes. Then it trailed off and trickled away.

He said, "Perverted?" And looked into her eyes. "To suggest that my plan is the plan of a pervert, you have wounded me deeply. I want to ask you, if I am such a pervert, what does that say about you, being part of my plan?"

"That! Is none of your business." And she was right to say this, because she had no other comeback.

"I would say that you, Anya, are a pervert, too. But really, we both seem to enjoy expunging your innocence by doing these bad things, so who really cares?"

"You're right. If it makes us happy, how bad can it be?"

They stopped talking. There was a minute of silence, at the end of which they both knew it was time. "Are you going to expunge more of my innocence?" she asked with a small, vulnerable voice.

"Only if you ask me nicely," he replied with a devilish voice.

"Please, James, please! Please expunge more of my innocence," she cried as though in pain from want of having her innocence expunged.

"The pleasure is all mine, my queen."

"And mine as well. Think of it as a collaboration," she affirmed.

He rose from the chaise lounge love nest, held out his hand, and helped her to her feet. He turned her towards the mirror so he could see her reflection, and she his. He nuzzled her ear and dragged his lips across her neck, turning her towards him, kissing her on the mouth, which tasted like apricot blossoms. He pulled her sweater over her head, mussing her hair, exposing her from her shoulders to belly, her breasts hiding behind her brassiere as though they were embarrassed. Her breath quickened as he slid his hand to her shoulder and pushed forward the straps, pushing them down her forearms. He reached for the hook of her bra and unfastened it. She placed her hands on the cups, holding them in place, in a way, resisting him, as though she had lost her nerve. He pulled he hands away and the bra fell. She raised her hands to hide, but he stopped her and guided her hands to her hips, where he firmly held them until she relented, playful in her surrender. She pinkened, expressing a desire that was further fanned by the reflection in the mirror of his eyes feeding on the image of her body. Her areolae crinkled, becoming ruffles of pink, like carnations. She looked upward and rolled her head to his. He planted a long, moist kiss on the side of her neck. She felt his hands unzip her skirt, loosen the waist, and push it downward until it fell to the floor. He gently tugged at her underwear until it, too, fell. She stepped out of them, flinging them to the side with a foot. While she stood nude, reflected in the mirror, in front of her lover, she shyly covered her 'tantalesca-rosa' with a hand. His hands shook with excitement as he stripped off his clothes and tossed them to the side.

They stood together, reflected in the mirror, admiring each other until they swooned, melting into each other, becoming an offering; a prayer.

CHAPTER 9

When Anya and James first met, Anya was very inexperienced. She had had a single boyfriend near the end of her senior year in college. His name was Jean-Luc. Jean-Luc was French and spent a single semester at San Francisco State, studying abroad in America. He was eighteen-years-old. She was twenty-two. Their relationship began with flirtations. An obsessive crush followed, and then awkward dates, which led to continuous kissing and touching, and finally an explosion of blissful, innocent sex.

She discovered that she loved making love, but that she savored it shyly, feeling full passion, but not rendering it forth with the sounds or gestures of love because she found this humiliating, and so instead she endured her passion in noble silence. Afterwards, they stayed beneath the sheets, under which he would sneak peeks at her and she would allow the peeks if they were short enough. She found that many were too long, and so she would end them with a disapproving huff and pause the peeping game as a punishment, sometimes for even a few minutes, before it all began again.

The briefness of their relationship prevented them from exploring the ruder ways of physical love, and so she was very inexperienced.

Their relationship started in May and ended in June when Jean-Luc returned to France. They both suffered terribly at first, each sending a flood of emails and selfies, but, of course, no sexting; the thought of which never occurred to either of them.

After a month or so, his emails slowed to a trickle, and then stopped altogether. She sent several unanswered emails declaring her feelings for him. When there was no reply, she felt he had dumped her, which so wounded her pride that she hated all men for at least a few weeks.

After recovering from her hatred of men, her desire for Jean-Luc returned, starting as a trickle, then becoming a torrent which tormented her each night with erotic dreams that filled her with pleasure as well as guilt. The problem was exacerbated by the fact that he had jilted her, which invalidated the sincerity of their love, leaving nothing more to it than physical desire. She was ashamed.

After making love that night, James and Anya unfolded the comforter they kept near the chaise lounge. They pulled it over them and watched the fire burn low, becoming blue curling flames licking orange ambers. He rolled away from her and fell asleep. She could not sleep. Her mind pulsed with rhythm and rhyme, so she slipped away, threw on a robe, and went to the loft to write down the words, parapgraphlets, and puns that flitted by. She was having a wordgasm, a time during which she wrote down what came to her, hot and raw, unfiltered, ungrammatical, and misspelled.

She sat at her desk in the loft, switched on her iMac, and began typing her musings into Shards as though tapping out code. Occasionally, she paused and stared into space with her eyes closed so she could focus on the elusive echoes that crept through her mind. Then she would open her eyes and madly type. Tonight, this is what she wrote:

Anika felt excitement touched with dread because this was that one night each month that she promised to give herself to him totally, to let him have her as he wanted, without any regard for the legitimacy of their love. Although she never knew exactly what to expect, she knew he would request love from her with a tone of voice that was coarse and raw and would abrade the surface of her soul, laying bare deeper layers of sensation, exposed and tingling, making her shiver.

She would encourage him by burying her face into his neck and with other non-verbal cues, choosing carefully from a vernacular of unspoken gestures. This was how she liked to start, but as they progressed, she would add sighs, whimpers, and cries, then a word, and then two words, until words began to spill out of her. He would re-avow his love for her with his own words and this allowed them both to pursue it with complete abandon.

Tonight, he took her hand and led her to a room whose four walls, ceiling, and floor were covered with mirrors. A six-sided, internally reflecting cube exponentially multiplied their images into the millions. She watched the reflections while her lover undressed her, unbuttoning, unzipping, tugging at straps that slid across her skin, peeling away garments, which he dropped to the floor. After each fell away, he stopped and looked into her eyes, kissed her cheeks and lips, and then returned with renewed deliberation to the task at hand. As he unbuttoned, unhooked, and unzipped, a river of thoughts flowed through her mind, each slightly different, each arousing a different synapse and fiber.

Anya stopped writing, smiled with satisfaction, and said to herself, "Simple, tawdry, kinky, perfect." She then read her writing, correcting grammar, changing words, and embellishing until she had no more energy. She returned to the living room, which had grown cold as the fire had died. She sat by James on the chaise lounge and watched him sleep. James was her muse and her love for him spawned wordgasms and fragments of stories that spilled out of her. "I just love you, James. I am just… in love with you. I love you and I will always love you. I can't help it." She dropped her robe, slipped beneath the comforter, and slid into the nook made by the arch of his body where she fell asleep.

CHAPTER 10

Feo's studio was south of Market, near Third and Bryant, in San Francisco; a part of the city rarely visited by James and Anya. It was in a warehouse made of cinder blocks, corrugated aluminum and a mosaic of dirt-plastered reinforced windows. It had a bare cement floor and a worn beige rug near the center. Florescent lights hung from rafters. The walls had little insulation. Two electric space heaters warmed the studio. Rats foraged there and prominently left droppings, marking territory. Feo had been there for years and had upgraded it, adding a small bedroom, kitchenette, bathroom, tub, and hot water.

After meeting with James and Anya, Isabella and Feo drove away from the studio in her green Prius, which floated silently down Market towards the Castro district. Feo sat in the passenger seat. As they drove, the wet air outside turned from fog, to mist, to drizzle, spritzing the windshield with droplets and then became fog again.

The sound of James' voice echoed in Feo's mind and sounded like a barking dog. It annoyed him and he blocked it out. His thoughts turned to Anya and the delicate shape of her foot and lower leg, which he had touched as he knelt before her. Her redolence cloaked him in a cloud, settled on him like dew and stayed on his fingertips, which he rubbed together and brought to his nose. The odor set off a swarm of impressions that buzzed through his mind like the violins in *El Amor Brujo*, until he realized it was playing on the radio.

Isabel spoke, calling him Carlo, a variation of his given name, Carlos. "What do you think of him, Carlo?"

"*Extraño.*"

"*Como?*"

"His fears, his obsession,"

"His obsession?"

"He's obsessed by his woman."

"A woman is a common obsession, no?"

"No, not like this. This is deep, *profundo*. It rules him the way instinct rules a dog and he does not even know it. All he knows is constant torment and he seeks a cure from it."

"That's *loco*. They should be in therapy."

"*Si, son locos*, but there is also pleasure with their pain. He endures the pain to obtain the pleasure of his love for this woman. He is happy in his struggle. In a way, he is making a myth of himself, a myth he tells himself each day, embellishing it with each retelling. She loves him and likes the indulgence. They are indulging themselves in love. But beneath their love…" He trailed off.

"'*Debajo de su amor*'. It is lyrical to say it this way. *¿No?*"

"*Si.*"

"Tell me about *El debajo.*"

"Beneath their love, she represents life, she is life. It is his fear of death that causes him to seek life, to seek her. How funny it is that he would come to me to solve his problem."

"*Sí, qué irónico*. What do you think of her?" she asked.

"She is very committed to him, but she is conflicted, nervous, uncomfortable. It is a struggle and she is suffering."

"Should I draw up a contract?"

"Yes. Make it seventy-five thousand."

"Seventy-five thousand dollars? I thought it was sixty."

"We did not agree on a price. Make it Seventy-five thousand. I know this man. He will pay it."

They finished talking and became silent, leaving Feo alone with his thoughts. He sank into them deeply and soon felt twinges of grief that grew into mild nausea, a nausea he knew well. The cause of the grief was fated and could not have been avoided. It happened when he was a child. It was a time when he felt like dying. For months afterward, he never left his room, not even to use the third floor toilet shared by fifteen or so other boarders. Instead, he used a pot kept beneath the bed, which made the bedroom the family shared stink. They lived in a *barrio* in Los Angeles. It was in the summer. It was hot. He was ten years old.

Towards the end of this dark era, he chose the name Feo for himself, changing it from Carlos. *Feo* means ugly in Spanish. He also got a skull tattoo on his shoulder to remind him of his brush with death and how a large part of him had died. The new name and tattoo gave him unexpected relief and felt similar to the relief felt by those who cut themselves. However, the relief was small compared to the darkness, which at times swallowed everything. Nightly, he dreamt of playing soccer with friends in the street and of flirting with Cecilia in Sunday school, and her black hair, coffee-colored face, and black eyes, and then the dream would end and he would again experience the pain of having sight ripped away. It destroyed his ego and crushed his very self into nothing – even less than nothing.

It was not his parent's fault that he went blind. They were a family of illegal aliens living in a *barrio* making less than minimum wage. They had few options when Carlos became sick with yet another eye infection. The infection had always gone away before, but this time it persisted. Fluids ran from his eyes, and dried, becoming a crust that glued them shut. He ran a high fever.

They could not afford a doctor, and instead went to a healer who earned a few dollars reading palms and Tarot cards. She was called *La Bruja* out of fear, but also respect by those who used her services to portend the future, or to cast spells so they could find work or love, or to cast spells on others, often a former boss or lover. They paid *La Bruja* with nickels and dimes because that was all they had.

She practiced her sorcery in a darkened den filled with incense smoke, near Sixth and Temple in downtown Los Angeles. It was down an alley, beneath a stairway, and behind a black door, which led into an old brick building. The walls of her den had posters of the Virgin and Child, mirrors shaped like crucifixes, and black and white photos of adobe churches, weddings, brides, grooms, old women, and young children. There was a bookshelf covered with Day of the Dead figurines. Strings of colored lights hung from the ceiling. The *Bruja* was Chilean.

As they entered, his mother admonished him to be good because, "We don't want to offend the spirits." But as they stepped through the door, Carlos mistook a plume of incense smoke for a ghost and stopped in his tracks. He was terrified, but remained stoic because ten-year-old Mexican males are not permitted to cry. So, instead of crying, he glared at the smoke with anger and contempt, using the same face he made to frighten away dangers that arose in life, like an angry dog, or a bully, or a ghost in the form of smoke.

"Come, Carlos. Please." His mother was firm.

Carlos saw *La Bruja* standing behind a curtain of beads, staring at him. She looked worried and somehow, he knew that he had already offended the spirits by treating the ghost with the same disrespect that he did a dog or a bully. He glanced back at the incense wick, but the smoke was gone. It was too late.

La Bruja emerged from behind the beads. She was short, brown, and wrinkled. She had gray hair pulled back into a severe bun. Her lilac perfume mingled with the incense. She wore a purple cotton dress. She snatched his hand and stared at the palm with the focus of a doctor examining a patient. She closed her eyes and laid a hand across his forehead. They stayed like this for minutes until she said, "Sit," and gestured at a chair by a table.

They sat. She dealt cards, pausing after each to calculate its meaning. She took his hand again and stared into it, while holding her breath, sitting motionlessly for minutes. She arose from the chair, shuffled around the table to him, placed her forehead against his and stared into his eyes. Carlos felt her presence seep into him. It gripped his heart with cold fingers until everything went dark.

The next thing he knew, he was home in the bedroom he shared with his family. His mother brought him a mug on a tray and set it by the bed. "*La Bruja* said you will be all right. Drink this tea. It will fight the spirits in your eyes."

The tea sedated him and he fell asleep. When he awoke the next day, he could not see because he had gone blind. During the months that followed, he suffered so terribly that it would be a sin to repeat the ordeal of his pain. Because it was in the past and there was nothing he could do and he didn't consciously dwell on it, but his unconsciousness did, and it regularly welled up and overflowed into his conscious mind. The nausea he felt now, while he rode home with Isabel, recurred weekly, sometimes lasting for minutes, sometimes lasting for days and sleepless nights.

As they continued down Market towards Feo's home in the Castro, Feo stewed in his trauma. He could not face the night alone. He needed to be with his lover. He needed to touch her, to smell her, to hear her voice, and converse with her. She never failed to transform depression into hope and sometimes joy. Her name was Dana. He texted her, 'I will be home soon. Are you free? Can you come by?'

She replied, 'Let's have dinner, tequila and tacos? How does Tacolicious sound?'

'*Perfecto*, see you there. I'll be there in 15,' he texted back to her and then said, "Isabel, can you drop me at Tacolicious? I am meeting Dana there."

Being blind, he knew Dana through his four remaining senses, particularly touch. He knew the shape of her oval face, high cheekbones, rising forehead, and full lips. He knew the feel of her soft hair that curled into ringlets around his fingers and falling to her delicate shoulders. Her body tapered from shoulders to belly and then widened to her hips, tapering again to her thighs and calves. She was voluptuous, soft, and warm and gave him sanctuary from his sorrow.

CHAPTER 11

Later that same night, after Anya and James had endured their humiliation in Feo's studio, long after they had arrived home, made love, and fallen asleep, James awoke. The fire had burned out and the room had gone cold. He was warm beneath the comforter beside Anya, on the chaise lounge. She slept, curled up in the crescent of his body, softly snoring. He pressed himself to her backside, reached over her, and placed his palm on her belly, a position he stayed in for minutes, weighted down by contentment. He finally moved to a new position, propping himself up on an elbow so he could see her face. He moved his hand from her belly to her breasts, and then to her face, which he touched with the back of his hand. He was happy, content, and at peace.

He disentangled himself from her, slipped out of bed, disappeared into the darkness, and returned with a chair, which he placed by the chaise lounge, near the spent fire. While he watched her sleep, he began to recall their first tryst, which had occurred on their sixth date. Until then, she had avoided intimate settings. James noticed her reticence and respected this unspoken boundary. It was on a Friday evening after they had spent that afternoon hiking in Mount Tamalpais State Park. The butterflies, blossoms, and bright yellow banana slugs were out in full bloom that day. After hiking to Stinson Beach and back, they returned to their respective homes, showered, changed, and later met in Height Ashbury at the Siamese Lotus Blossom Café for dinner. After dinner, James said, "Let's go back to my place, drink a little wine, watch a movie... also, I have something for you – something I'd like to show you."

"Okay." She was ready to see his place and anticipated his suggestion by packing an overnight bag that she left in her car. She drove behind him, following in her car as they drove across town to the Marina. They parked in his garage and took the stairs from the garage to a short hallway, which passed by the laundry room and ended in the kitchen. From there, he took her on a quick tour of the first floor, which ended in the living room.

"We'll watch the movie in here. We can lay down on the chaise lounge. There are plenty of pillows. Make yourself comfortable."

She sat on the chaise lounge. He made a fire and then grabbed the control and turned on the TV, which stood to the right of the fireplace. The title page of the movie appeared on the screen. It was *The Mask of Dimitrios.*

Before he started the movie, he asked, "Wine?"

"Sure."

He hurried away, returning with two glasses, hers, a light Muscat that was chilled and bubbly, and his, a thirty-year tawny port. He handed her the Muscat and joined her on the chaise lounge, laying his left arm around her shoulders.

"To new beginnings," he said.

"Skoal," she replied and sipped. The wine was light and cool on her tongue, refreshing like ice tea. "Nice. What is it?"

"Muscat. Sweet, no?"

"Yes."

The Mask of Dimitrios is an obscure classic movie from the 1940s starring Peter Lorre and Sydney Greenstreet. It was a strange, campy, Noir story, in black and white. The story followed a trail littered with people Dimitrios had betrayed. It took them from Istanbul, to Athens, Belgrade, and Paris. They loved the queerness of Peter Lorre and the beady eyed, fat-man, Sydney Greenstreet, who dressed in a bowler hat and trench coat. He was consumed by hatred for Dimitrios and obsessed with revenge.

While they watched the film, a storm blew outside, whipping water from whitecaps on the bay and splattering it against windowpanes, making it perfect weather to be warm inside, watching an old movie in front of a fire. She lay across him, her back on his chest, his arms encircling her. He periodically tipped his head to hers, touching her forehead with a cheek. She took his hand and wove their fingers together, only to disentangle them and let go of his hand, taking it again minutes later, and weaving the fingers back together again.

The movie ended and an awkward silence followed, as they both pondered the uncertainties that lay between where they were at that moment and the intimacy that they would embrace for the first time. He broke the tension. "Another glass?" She nodded, and he disappeared into the kitchen.

She sat upright on the chaise lounge, propped up by pillows with her arms tightly crossed and legs straightforward, her right leg crossing her left at the ankle. *Of course, there will be some sort of seduction process. Like this second glass of wine. S*he put her glasses on.

He returned. "Here, it's a Viognier." He handed it to her and then disappeared again, leaving her alone on the lounge while she sipped.

"Citrusy, no?" she heard him say from some place in the house.

"Yes, wonderful. None for you?"

"No, thanks."

"How long have you had this house?"

"My grandfather bought it. He willed it to me when I was ten. I moved in on my own when I was around twenty-three, after college. My parents live in Switzerland. I stay here. They stay there. Haven't seen them in years."

He returned and put on music and then plopped down next to her.

And now a little night music, she nodded knowingly as though she had expected it.

"How's the wine?"

She cocked her head, raised a doubtful eyebrow and looked him in the eye. "Do you give all your *friends* wine when they visit you on this chaise lounge?"

"This chaise lounge? It's new. Got it last month. You're my first visitor. How do you like it?"

She liked it all very much — the music, the wine, the fire — but she felt insecure. "It's okay."

"I'll be right back. I have to show you something." He disappeared again, leaving her alone with butterflies in her belly.

He returned in a flash. "Here, let me show you." He sat by her cross-legged, cradling a photo album in his lap. "This is my collection of you." He opened it and on the first page was a photograph of her, taken at the labyrinth in Golden Gate Park. "I've kept them all. These are my favorites."

The first photo in the album caught surprise rippling across her face.

The next photo was of her sitting on a bench, her eyes focused on a crumpled yellow paper, her brows, semicircles of concentration.

"This is the first picture I took of you. Remember? In the park? You read a poem."

They turned the page. The next was of her at the Sutro Baths, standing on the wall over the beach, waves, fog, and sea in the background. There was one that was out of focus, colors blurred together like an impressionist painting. The pictures showed Anya the diversity of herself as seen by someone else: faces in solemn repose, others playful and laughing. All meticulously printed, mounted, and framed. She was charmed. "They're beautiful," she emoted and then blushed at the conceit of her comment.

"They are beautiful, and you are beautiful."

He put the album aside and leaned towards her. He removed her glasses and brought his face up to hers, his lips near hers, but she turned away as though one last obstacle remained. He hesitated, and then moved his mouth to hers again and they kissed.

He removed the pillows, gently tipped her back into a laying position. He moved his upper body up and over her. He methodically explored the form of her face with his lips, each dip and curve, the corners of her mouth, the bend of her brow, the flicker of a lash. He savored her aroma, which reminded him of roses. She loved his touch, but remained silent in her pleasure, afraid to be observed by her inner-voyeur who snickered at her.

They stayed like this for endless minutes, savoring each grain of time and space, until he took hold of her shirt and untucked it. He slid a warm hand beneath it, onto her abdomen, which caused her to gasp. He paused. Her eyes were closed; her face, relaxed. They invited him to continue, so he did, moving his second hand beneath her shirt. After a few minutes of exploring this new intimacy, he began to lift her shirt up over her head, but she stopped him.

She slid beneath the comforter and pulled off her shirt and handed it to him, and then put a hand over her mouth and smirked. He removed his shirt and joined her beneath the comforter, pressing his chest against hers, allowing them to feel the contours of each other's bodies for the first time. They kissed madly, and within moments, he stripped away the rest of her clothing.

Their first intimacy was brief, lasting less than a minute, but it was enough to make them officially lovers. Afterward, she lay beneath him, staring into his eyes, basking in the afterglow while he touched her face with his lips. Eventually, he rolled away from her and out from beneath the comforter. He stood over her, looking down, naked in the flickering fire light. She admired his body and thought he was beautiful and wanted to touch him, but would not dare. He began to lift the comforter, but she grabbed it and held it tight. He respected her modesty and stopped.

"Should we go out for a walk?" he asked.

"Okay."

"I'm going to shower first. Want to join me?"

She shook her head 'no' and he felt rejected. "Okay, suit yourself." He disappeared.

Once he left, she pulled on her shirt and jeans and found her way to the bathroom. The door was open, but she knocked anyway. "Change your mind?" he asked.

"No, but I do need a shower. Perhaps, when you're done?"

"A little shy, aren't we?" he said in a friendly way.

She winced and repeated. "When you're done."

"No problem."

When he was done, he stepped out of the shower and stood facing her, giving her a full frontal view of his body. He took a towel and dried while she watched. She liked looking at him.

"It's all yours," he said, referring to both the shower and his body.

"Thank you." She shut the door behind him.

The next morning after their first night together, they arose early and decided to exercise. James changed into running shorts, shirt, and shoes. Anya wore the jeans and cotton shirt she wore the night before. She rode a touring bike James kept in the garage. Her red hair was pulled back into a ponytail that flipped back and forth as she pedaled. James jogged alongside. They headed down Scott Street to the Marina and turned left, jogging past the Palace of Fine Arts, Saint Francis Yacht club, and on to Fort Point and the Goldengate Bridge. From there, they circled back home. They showered, separately, because of her unnatural modesty, and then dressed.

"Time for brunch," he announced. "I know where to go."

"Where?"

"The Grand Hyatt. The 36th floor."

He grabbed his camera while she called an Uber. It was a fifteen minute ride to the Grand Hyatt Hotel, which sat at the corner of Sutter and Stockton, just north of Union Square. There they had brunch, high above the city, overlooking the bay, which that morning was filled with sailboats whose spinnakers dotted the grey-blue water with bright colors. They ate smoked salmon, cream cheese, capers on toast, and shared a single glass of Champaign, the whole time chatting away, oblivious to their surroundings. She described life on the ranch with dreamy detachment. "I had a dog, Ms. Barkley, who had a very good sense of humor. When I was young, we played tirelessly. She died when I was in high school. Leslie was my best friend. She lived miles away. We would ride bikes to see each over. Buelton... such a small town. We had pet parades, picnics on the Fourth of July, and a Christmas tree in the center of town. Pea Soup put us on the map. We're famous for it. There are signs up and down the freeway for Pea Soup. It's pretty corny. In Buelton, life is slow, secure, comfortable, set in its ways. Nothing ever changes. I had so many long, summer days with nothing to do but hike through the green fields and daydream. I was ready to leave and come to the big city." She described how she adapted to the jolting chaos of city life when she went to university, and how she loved the diversity of the people, the intellectual stimulation of everything, and of being free from the constraints of the ranch and her controlling father. She planned to stay. "And besides, I can go back anytime I want," she said. "And now, I live with two married men who are my close friends. My father doesn't know. He'd think it was strange. When I lived in Buelton, I had read about gay people, but didn't know anyone like that, at least, that's what I thought. I thought there just weren't any gay people in Buelton and that I'd never know a gay person, ever, in my life.

"But thinking back now, there was a small ranch called the Hayden House Ranch. It was hidden away in a grove of oak trees. Two men lived there. When I was a kid, I just thought they lived with each other, but looking back, I can see they were 'together'. I knew one of them pretty well. Danny. He was my friend. He was gay. I had no idea. So, what about you?"

James said, "Well, I've had a pretty good time; my whole life, really. I've done what I want, basically, at my own pace, apart from the crowd, not exactly alone, but always a distance away from everyone else. I do my guitar business. I go to auctions to buy, and trade shows to sell. I make the brochures. I photograph the guitars and write down all their details. I have a web site where I advertise them. I choose the fonts and colors for the brochures. I get a few printed for the shows. When it comes to real work, I have to say I've never done any. I've played most of my life. Never had to take things seriously. I'm lucky, I guess."

He told her about Jack Hooker, his best friend. "The man who keeps me sane," and how he had known him since Freshman Year in High School. "He's been my best friend for fourteen years — half my life. I sort of grew up with him. We went off to college the same year. I took a little longer, six years." He blushed, as though he'd been caught red-handed. *Oh, shit. She'll think I'm stupid.*

"It took me five and a half, if you include junior college," she said, and he felt better about it.

"Back then, I didn't know what I wanted to do. Still don't know."

"I want to write."

"Lucky you."

They took extraordinary care when speaking to each other, thoughtfully choosing their words so as not to offend. They listened with interest, holding onto each word, patiently waiting for the next. She laughed at his jokes and groaned at his puns, and suggested that he suffered from 'punis envy', and then watched his quizzical face while waiting for the pun to sink in. When it didn't, she added, "Like penis envy. You know … Sigmund Freud."

"Oh, I get it now."

They could not stop touching each other, and behaved like teenagers, besotted, shamelessly kissing for all to see, as their hearts beat aloud for all to hear. In this way, they animated the ambiance of the restaurant. Everyone smiled at them. Their conversation turned from themselves to the view of the boats in the bay, and then to the others in the restaurant.

"Are they all looking at us?" Anya whispered.

"Holy shit! They are," he whispered back.

One man held up a glass and nodded, as if toasting them. James and Anya glowed with embarrassment and looked away. "Let's get out of here." James asked for the check.

After brunch, they strolled down Stockton Street to Union Square. Once they reached the square, they stepped up the few steps from the sidewalk into the park, passing by a heart-shaped sculpture brightly painted with a forest of red woods, grazing deer, and banana slugs. She posed with the heart and he took a picture. As they walked between the palm trees and neatly trimmed hedges, they mingled with the micro-culture of the park: a juggler, a mime, a man playing bongos, a woman sketching portraits, a couple selling belt buckles made of thinly sliced, polished geodes. The central plaza of Union Square was tiled with gray and pink granite. At the center stood a four-story tall Greek column with a bronze statue of a woman perched on top. Anya read the placard at the base, "Dewey Monument, a war memorial from the Spanish-American war. 1903. The statue symbolizes victory."

Anya said, "I have to go soon. I'm tutoring François at two."

"Gee, uh, when will I see you again? How about tonight?"

"No, not tonight."

"Tomorrow? Sunday? I'm going to a guitar auction in Burlingame. Want to come?"

She paused, and then said, "Sure."

"Great! It starts at one-thirty. I'll pick you up around noon."

She hailed a cab. "See you tomorrow, James."

CHAPTER 12

The next day, James pulled up and parked in front of Anya's place in Twin Peaks. He texted her, 'I'm here,' and waited in his Porsche.

'Coming,' she texted back.

A moment later, the front door opened. Roger stood in the doorway, arms crossed with a dismayed look on his face.

"Oh, no," James mumbled.

Anya appeared at the door, stepped around Roger, and trotted over to the car. She opened the door and got in.

"Quick. Let's go." But before James could drive off, Roger appeared by her door and knocked on the window.

"Oh, boy," James said, and lowered the window.

"I'm not going to ask why she didn't come home last night."

"Yes, Roger, please, don't ask," she replied

"And I'm not going to ask whether you used a condom."

"OH, MY GOD!" She exploded.

"Dude, you're a tiny bit over the line. It's okay. I know how to treat a lady."

"He does, Roger. Goodbye." She closed the window. "God, I'm really embarrassed."

"Strange, are you like his first child or something?" James started the engine and carefully pulled out of the parking spot.

"He's a little intrusive."

"Yes, he is."

"Well, more than intrusive, really annoying."

"A bit. At some point, he might try my patience, but he hasn't yet."

She changed the subject. "I'm so excited. I've never been to an auction before."

"Yeah, this should be pretty good. Some of the things they're going to sell were seized by the police from criminals. Some are from bankruptcies. Some from estates. The guitar I want should be on the block at around one-thirty. It came from an estate of a guy who died. Someone I knew."

"Oh, my. Sorry to hear. A friend?"

"No, but an acquaintance. His name was Henry Clydeborn. He was a collector, but he didn't collect guitars. His collecting had no real focus at all, actually. I think he just liked buying things. I met him at an auction and we hit it off. I told him about rare guitars, the next thing I knew, he wanted to show me his stuff at his place in Atherton. Man! That was a weird evening! He was a weird guy. He lived on Ridgeview. Hedges, ten feet high, hid the house from the street."

As James spoke, the events of that evening unfolded in his mind. He recalled seeing Henry's plantation style house: the dormer windows on the third floor and an observatory on the top of the house, looming over the hedges.

He stopped in front of the gate and texted Henry, 'I'm here.' The gate opened and the full house came into view. It was huge. Two-story tall columns ran the length of it. Both the first and second floors had large porches. The house was white and had paned windows with green shutters on both the first and the second floor. The grounds were grassy and the gardens manicured. The driveway circled around a rose garden in front of the house. A flagpole stood in the center without a flag. He parked and ambled over to the first floor porch and up a short flight of stairs to the front door, which was open. A housekeeper waited at the door.

"Mr. Clydeborn is in the living room. Please, come with me."

She led him into an expansive living room. Henry sat in a purple brushed-cotton wingback. He was dressed in a felt robe, white pajamas, and slippers. He had white hair, a white mustache, pale blue eyes and a white face that looked stretched from plastic surgery.

The image of Henry faded and James continued to describe the evening. "Yeah, he was really strange," James said to Anya. "He told me he had three acres and that his house was like ten thousand square feet. He had a greenhouse full of exotic plants. I remember him pointing to a huge pitcher plant and saying, '*Nepenthes Mirabilis*. A carnivorous plant. Sometimes I feed it flies. Sometimes frogs and newborn mice."

"Good God!"

"Yeah, I know, really gross. Henry was really fat. Morbidly obese, I'd say. Rotund. A huge gut. Short. He was also out of breath, gasping for air just walking across the room. He perspired a lot and was always damp. His skin had the pallor of an addict. I learned later he was an addict who took methadone every day. Still, he managed the affairs of his life, which consisted mostly of eating and buying and of massive hedonism that took place at secluded whorehouses in the middle of desserts in Nevada. I heard that he spent tens of thousands a year at places like that, on binges that lasted days, days without sleep, high on cocaine and other drugs. There, in a whorehouse, he could have everything he craved, unrestrained, anonymously, without consequence. At least, that's what he thought. He died of throat cancer. I'll bet he got it from whoring. You know … human papilloma virus."

"That's disgusting."

"Yeah, he was disgusting, but he had some cool stuff. He showed it to me: dinosaur bones, meteorites, rare coins, African masks, and a couple of classic cars. I told him about guitars and The Fool, a rare guitar that was coming up for auction that I wanted. He wanted to know all about it.

"Before I left that evening, he disappeared for around ten minutes, when he came back, he was visibly stoned, slurring his words, unsteady on his feet. He was a very sick man."

"When I went to the auction, The Fool had been pulled from the program. I found out later that he had bought it days earlier. Can you believe that?"

"That's psychopathic."

"He was psychopathic! He was spoiled and selfish. He belittled and used the people around him and they seemed to hate him for it. He was glutinous, obese, burly, rude, impatient, and always sweating. A truly repulsive individual."

"What about the guitar?"

"Right! The Fool. It's awesome. It's a 1961 Gibson SG Standard that was hand painted by an award-winning painter, Rick Daskam. He painted it to look exactly like Eric Clapton's famous psychedelic Gibson. Its fingerboard is Brazilian Rosewood with inlaid mother of pearl fret markers. It has twin pickups and a list of hidden numbers, signatures, and dates, like the one inside the 'neck pickup cavity', a signature - J.K.

1997. Eric Clapton owned it. He gave it to George Harrison, who, in turn, gave it to Todd Rungren. It's been owned by Rock 'n' Roll Royalty. It's a Royal Guitar. I think I can sell it in Japan for more than thirty thousand dollars."

He paused, and then asked, "So, you've never been to an auction before?"

"No, I haven't."

"How would you like to do the bidding for me?"

"Don't be silly."

"You can do it. It's easy. There is an opening bid, which for The Fool is three thousand. And then there are incremental bids of three hundred dollars. If you want to bid, you hold up the paddle, which has my number on it. You can also call out a price that is more than the increment."

"How do I know when to bid?"

"I'll tell you."

"Okay. I think I can do that."

"Oh, there is another little detail. I'm not going to be present during the bidding."

"What?"

"Yeah. It's a little subterfuge. The guys who buy and sell guitars all know each other and they know me. I want to play a little trick on them to gain an advantage."

"How will I know what to bid if you're not there?"

"I will be there, listening in on your cell phone. You put on an earpiece, call me, and then put the phone in your purse. No one will know. I'll be able to hear what's going on. When I say 'bid', you do it. Do you think you can do that?"

"Yeah, I think so."

"Good. So, when we get there, you go in first. I want you to go to the display where The Fool is. I want you to hold it, examine it, to kvell over it, say you want it, say you must have it, and then leave. They will see you. They'll think you're a novice."

"What does 'kvell' mean?"

"It means to excessively emote. Do you think you can do that?"

"Yeah, I think I can."

"After you leave, I will go in and inspect the guitar. I'm going to say it's a fake and that I'm not interested and then I'll leave. Before it's auctioned, call me, hide the phone and we'll do it."

The Hilton Bayfront Hotel in Burlingame sits next to Anza Lagoon, which empties into the bay near Bayfront Park, on a strip of land that's bordered on three sides by the bay, an estuary, and a tiny inlet that connects them. Water flows through the channel as the tide rises and falls. It's an airport hotel, a few miles from the San Francisco Airport, close enough for the roar of jet engines to drown out all sound. Airport visitors stay there: pretty Asian stewardesses, Americans returning from vacations, some wearing Hawaiian shirts and leis, as well as businessmen in slacks and fitted shirts with laptops, sitting at the bar, drunken, blabbing with the bartender, living life on the road.

James entered the parking structure, but before parking, he stopped and said, "Now, you jump out. Find the Spinnaker room. That's where The Fool is. Don't forget. You need to Kvell."

"Kvell, to emote. Okay."

"I'll meet you there, but we'll pretend not to know each other. Got it?"

"Got it."

She walked from the parking structure, across a parking lot to the circular driveway by the lobby where guests left cars with valets. The lobby opened into an expansive, two-story high inner space that was filled with sofas, chairs, coffee tables, and people. Signs directed her to the auction, which had taken all of the rooms on the east wing of the hotel.

There were ten or so separate displays of auction items and around twenty people examining the goods. She saw The Fool, but did not go right to it. She wanted to be less obvious. She decided to look through the goods. Near The Fool was a display of jewelry where she busied herself for several minutes, trying on necklaces and examining brooches, complaining that they were all too expensive, and then she moved onto The Fool. She pretended that she had stumbled upon it and that it was love at first sight and that she wanted it. "Oh, my god. What is that?" She pointed to the brightly colored guitar.

"It's called The Fool."

"It's beautiful. Is it a real instrument or just some sort of novelty?"

"I would say it's both. My name is John, may I tell you about The Fool?"

"Please."

"Uh, what is your name?"

"Anya."

"Are you a guitar collector?"

"No, I'm staying here and wanted to see what was going on. I've never been to an auction before."

"So, you don't collect."

"No, but this is really cool. Please, tell me about it."

"Well, it's a Gibson Standard from 1961. It was painted by a famous artist who gave it to Eric Clapton."

"Eric Clapton! I love Eric Clapton."

"The artist was Rick Daskam."

"Never heard of him."

"Well, he was a well-known painter of wildlife. Would you like to hold it? I'll take it out of the case." He gently lifted the guitar, holding it up, giving her a full-frontal view of the abstract designs in pastel blue, red, green and yellow. "What do you think?"

"Wow!" she said. He handed it to her. "Gee, kind of heavy. Do you think he played it?"

"Most definitely. And so did George Harrison."

"The Beatle! You're kidding! That's amazing!"

"Yep. Eric gave it to George."

"Wow. Well, I'm interested. What's the opening bid?"

"Three thousand dollars."

"Hmmm. That's a little on the pricey side for me, but I'm interested." She handed it back to John.

"We're taking it to the auction block at around one-thirty."

James arrived. "Hello," he said to John. "Ah, The Fool. I saw it in the catalog."

"My name is John. Are you a collector?"

"Yes, I am. Nice to meet you, John. Nice guitar."

"Have you heard of The Fool?"

"I have."

Anya said, "It was played by Eric Clapton and George Harrison!"

"Right. Do you have any proof of that?" James asked John.

"Well, we have this." John pointed to a photo of Eric Clapton holding the guitar. "And this, it's from the *Rolling Stone*." He produced a copy of *Rolling Stone* and turned to the page of the article.

James read it. "Uh huh. Well, maybe. Who was the last owner?"

"I am not at liberty to disclose that."

"Do you know what it sold for?"

"I don't."

"The opening bid is three thousand dollars? Something doesn't smell right."

"I beg your pardon?"

"I think it's a fake."

"It is not a fake."

"Well, to you it's not, but to me it is. I'm not interested. Good luck," he said and left.

A little before one-thirty, Anya dialed James on her cell phone. She put on an earpiece and put the phone in her purse.

"Can you hear me?" James asked.

"Yes."

"Where are you now?"

"Heading to the auction room."

"You may want to sit in the middle. You'll be less conspicuous there."

"All right."

Anya sat several rows back from the front by the aisle, paddle in hand, and waited for The Fool. After a few minutes, the auctioneer introduced the guitar.

"All right. The next item is number 194, a Gibson Guitar, owned by Eric Clapton and George Harrison. It was painted by the well-known artist Rick Daskam for Eric. The opening bid is three thousand dollars. Will anyone start the bidding?"

"Go ahead, open the bidding," James said and Anya raised her paddle.

"I have three thousand, from the lady, do I hear thirty-three hundred?" the auctioneer chattered away. Someone in the audience bid thirty-three hundred dollars, then thirty-six hundred dollars, then thirty-nine hundred dollars.

James said, "Let's wait and see who the other bidders are."

The bidding continued, reaching sixty-three hundred dollars. "All right, I have sixty-three hundred. Sixty-six hundred anyone? Come on, this is a famous guitar, owned by famous guitarists. Can I get sixty-five hundred?" Someone bid. "Okay I have sixty-five hundred. Anyone want to bid sixty-six hundred?" There was silence. "Okay, I have sixty-five hundred; going once, going twice."

"Now bid eight thousand," James said.

Anya raised her paddle. "Eight thousand."

"Wow, now there's someone who knows the value of a rare collectable like this. I now have eight thousand. Do I hear nine thousand?" There was silence. "How about eighty-five hundred?" Again, silence. "Eighty-one hundred, anyone? That's cheap for a piece of Rock 'N' Roll history." Silence followed. "Okay, eight thousand dollars… going once… going twice… sold to the lady for eight thousand dollars."

"Nice work. I'll meet you at the pickup station," James said.

CHAPTER 13

The memory of the auction and their first weekend together faded away and James found himself by the fire watching Anya sleep. His thoughts returned to the meeting with Feo earlier that evening. In his mind's eye, he could see Feo touching Anya and her pained look. A bolt of jealousy and guilt stabbed his gut.

"Oh, man, what am I doing?" He sat, head in hand, guilty over their project with Feo, when suddenly he remembered the dinner reservation at La Mar with Jack Hooker. "Oh, my God. We're going to be late!" He knelt over her, kissed her temple and she awoke. She smiled at him and he smiled back. "Sorry to wake you, but we're meeting Jack in forty-five minutes."

"Yikes," she yelped. She jumped from beneath the comforter and ran naked to the bathroom. Minutes later, they had showered, changed, and were on their way to La Mar for causas, empanadas, cebiche (con un 'b'), camarones, y pulpo. She had heard a lot about Jack, but had never met him. She knew he had dropped out of college his senior year and never went back, but did not know why.

James and Jack met in their first year of high school. They became best friends. Jack was a man who did not have everything, but he did have many things, some in overabundance. He excelled in high school, went to Stanford, and earned nearly straight A's until his senior year when he crashed and burned and then dropped out, never completing his degree. He was wealthy, but unlike James, he was self-made and his trade was marijuana. After dropping out, he founded a string of medical marijuana dispensaries in the Bay Area. He managed them for years until he sold them and made a fortune. He was also generous and had donated one million dollars to The People's Shelter for Women and Children in Oakland.

They drove down Embarcadero Avenue, through Fisherman's Wharf — passing the piers that began with Pier Forty-Three — and descended towards Pier One. Where Grant Avenue intersects Embarcadero, a streetcar track joins the avenue and runs down its center between the two lanes of traffic. Antique streetcars passed by with the click-clack of metal wheels rolling along steel rails. The streetcars were made in bygone eras in cities across the country, like Philadelphia and Kansas City. There they were scrapped and forgotten about, some rusting away in train cemeteries, a rare few rescued and housed in warehouses. The Market Street Railway Company, a non-profit organization, rescued them from oblivion and paid to have them refurbished, reupholstered, and painted, some with bright colors like fire engine red or banana yellow, others in subdued shades of green, blue, and gray. The Market Street Railway turned a small profit that they donated to feed the poor. As James and Anya drove, they passed pier buildings that opened up onto Embarcadero with arches two stories high, tall enough for the trains that would travel on tracks down Embarcadero to the Piers, turning away from the main track, onto a sidetrack that disappeared into the yawning mouths of Pier Building. There, they would load and unload cargo, to and from ships.

They arrived at La Mar at Pier 1½, a smaller pier that lies between Pier 1 and Pier 3. A sign hangs over the doorway of La Mar that reads, 'Cebicheria Peruana'. The façade of Pier 1½ is utilitarian, gray granite, all rectangles and right angles. It has two stories; the first consisting of picture windows that display store goods to pedestrians on the sidewalk and elaborate doorways that lead to shops. La Mar opened onto the sidewalk through oak doors and doorjambs made of black and green marble. The second story of Pier 1 ½ is a plain row of grated storm windows and gray stone; monotonous and repetitive.

James stopped in front of La Mar, jumped out of his car, and handed the keys to a valet who opened Anya's door and helped her to her feet. They strolled arm-in-arm into the restaurant where they found Jack Hooker at the bar sipping a drink. Jack was good looking, with brown hair combed to one side and blue eyes. Scar tissue pinched closed the outer corner of his left eye, and the pupil was enlarged.

"Hi, guys! Nice to finally meet you, Anya." Jack kissed her cheek and guided her to the seat next to him. James stood behind her, his hands on her shoulders.

"A drink before we eat, Anya?" Jack asked.

"Sure. What are you drinking?" Anya asked.

"Pisco Sour. It's Peruvian. Taste?" he said and offered her the glass.

"Why not?" She took the glass from his hand. It had a thick foam head that floated on the surface. "What's this frothy stuff?" she asked as she sipped.

"Lime juice, sugar, and a beaten egg white. It's Peruvian, like

Alpaca fur, or cebiche."

"I want one," Anya said.

"Bartender, one more," Jack said.

"Uh, two more," James added. He felt a little ignored and perhaps even a little jealous that his friend so adeptly captured her attention.

Anya and Jack chatted while James puzzled over the bartender, whose gender was ambiguous. The bartender had stylish, short-cropped hair dyed white, a slender but fit physique, and an Asian face that looked Vietnamese. The bartender wore boots, army fatigues, a sleeveless top, and a nose ring that pierced the septum. James speculated that he was a she, but was uncertain enough about it to be ready to change his mind. Nonetheless, language and the impersonal nature of the pronoun 'it' compelled him to assign a gender. *She was born a she,* he thought, so that was the pronoun he used.

"So, Anya, I've heard a lot about you. James says you're a writer. Have you published anything I've heard of?"

"Definitely not, but I've published a few short stories — a poem here and there — in the local paper."

"Like the *Santa Ynez Valley News* and once in the Lompoc *Record.*" James looked a little defensive. "It's a start. She's working on a novel."

"You write romance, I recall James saying."

"Yes…" She blushed and changed the subject. "What about you?"

"Me? Well, I'm looking at a new venture, in the drug trade."

"Pharmaceuticals?"

"Well, no, not exactly." Jack cleared his throat.

"Jack made his money in marijuana. He had medical marijuana dispensaries. He sold them all last year," James said.

"Perfectly legal," Jack added.

"Totally profitable," James said.

"An all-cash business. James wouldn't invest with me."

"I have ambiguous feelings about marijuana," James said.

"Look, I don't smoke anymore either, but medical marijuana is legal and lucrative. There's a demand, so why not?" Jack shrugged.

"Are you out of marijuana now?" she asked.

"I don't have any on me if that's what you mean."

"No, silly, I mean out of the business."

"Actually, I find myself again on that slippery slope, slowly sliding back in." Jack grinned self-consciously.

"Yeah, he has a big research project with Greg."

"Yeah, Greg, brilliant fellow that he is."

"A friend from high school. He's got a PhD in plant genetics. We're developing a new strain of pot, a GMO. You know, genetically engineered pot," James said.

"It's more potent, of course, but also without many of the other chemicals, so it has fewer side effects," Jack said.

"Like what?" Anya asked.

"Like drowsiness," Jack said.

"And overall stupidity," James said.

"Right, nearly all the chemicals leave your system in a few hours," Jack said.

"What about killing pain and things like that?" she asked.

Jack raised an eyebrow, smirked impishly and said, "Hmmm, hadn't really thought about that. But who cares? I'm going to give the people what they want."

Anya knitted her brows, rolled her eyes and shook her head. "I'll bet you smoke a lot, Jack"

"Actually I don't. I makes me paranoid"

"Yeah, Jack has a couple of skeletons in the closet that rise to the surface when he's under the influence. He's better off sober, believe me"

Jack nodded and shrugged his shoulders, conceding to James' point, and then said, ""I'm excited about it! It will be a new medical marijuana. A non-drowsy variety. I think a good brand name would be something like 'Look Alert'."

"That's ridiculous," she said.

"Well, I need a brand name. Something that isn't so, how do I say this, drug-oriented, you know, like 'Purple Haze' or 'Stoned Again'. Names like that are just not in good taste."

"Are you saying 'Look Alert' sounds classy?" she asked.

"Well, it's a little more socially acceptable than 'Super Green Crack', wouldn't you say?"

Anya gave him an incredulous look. She took a sip of her Pisco Sour. "I don't care for this anymore,"

James made a suggestion, "How about 'Vanilla Ice Cream'?"

"You want ice cream? We're just about to have dinner," said Jack, puzzled.

"No, Jack, he means as a name for your product," Anya said.

"Vanilla Ice Cream? Hmmm, hadn't thought of that one," Jack said.

"Or you can just put the pot directly into vanilla ice cream and sell it like that. Little ice cream cones of pot-infused Vanilla Ice Cream," James said.

"Vanilla Ice Cream and marijuana. That's really a good idea... I could sell it in Height Ashbury. Right next to Ben and Jerry's. Make a fortune."

"Yeah, you could call it Pleasant Dreams Ice Creams. It could become a franchise, build an empire. It would be bigger than McDonald's."

"Vanilla Ice Cream? As a recreational drug? What a heinous, corrupt thought. I don't like it at all." Anya smirked.

"Just think, Jack, you could go after the Recreational Drug Market for Children," James said.

"That is funny, but a bit heinous, isn't it?" Anya said.

"Yeah, I'll find another name."

Having exhausted the topic, they paused. Anya then said, "Excuse me, I need to run to the ladies room," and left.

"Was it something I said?" Jack asked James.

"No, I don't think so. I think she likes you."

"She's really pretty."

"And brainy and creative and funny and affectionate."

"You're in love."

"I am. I'm hooked, Hooker. She's astonishing," James said.

"So, tell me, what's so *astonishing* about her?"

"If you knew her the way I do, or should I say, if you knew anyone the way I know her, you would know that she is your destiny."

"Yeah, sure."

Anya returned just as the hostess appeared. "Your table is ready." She led them to a table at the back of the restaurant by a window that overlooked the bay. A waiter appeared with menus. "Anything to drink?"

"Water."

"Sparkling?"

"Please."

The waiter rattled off a list of specials. "I'll give you a few minutes to decide," he said and left.

"So, how long have you been dating?" Jack asked.

"Three months."

"James says you live together."

She looked uncomfortable. James put his arm around Anya and replied, "We do, and we're in love."

Anya relaxed, but Jack's face went slack as painful memories floated to the surface. James knew that Jack was thinking about Leena Kiraskaya and love lost. He broke the silence by saying, "Jack and I have known each other since we were fourteen. He's a very complicated fellow, my friend Jack."

"As is my friend James," Jack said.

"I'll drink to that. Complexity," James said.

"You know that he is rich, has never had to work, never suffered and struggled like the rest of us, lucky bastard that he is. Me, I've struggled."

Anya noticed Jack's damaged eye while saying, "He works. He trades in rare guitars."

"Yeah, right. I know about the guitar business. More of a pastime."

"I make good dough with guitars."

"I think you'd do it even if you lost money," Jack said. "Do you know where all his money comes from?"

She shook her head.

"His great-grandfather had patents in AM and FM radio, way back in the 1920s. That's how. Many are still used today and will probably always be used. One's called single-sideband modulation. No idea what it means, but they use it everywhere."

James pulled out his cell phone. "They use it in each cell phone."

"Because he doesn't have to work, he's at a loss to fill his time and he's terrified that life is dwindling away."

"I can tell you that having what you want all the time is really overrated," James said.

"He needs a little enthusiasm," Jack said.

"Oh, that's obvious." She took his hand. "Hopefully, I can help with that."

"How?"

"That's none of your business," she said.

"Well, you have writing, right? So, you sit down each day at your laptop and write, and re-read, and edit, and embellish, I guess," Jack said.

"Yes."

"So, you have something to do, and goals, and things like that, right?"

"Yes. I also tutor."

"Really, Jack didn't mention that. Tell me about it."

"I have a few kids — private school students. Their parents spend and spend on education, as if it will somehow buy them happiness."

"Does it?"

"For the parents, I think. Well, perhaps not happiness, but relief."

"What do you teach?"

"Writing, mostly. Sometimes I help with creative activities, like play writing or acting."

"I'll bet they pay well."

"They do," she said.

"She also tutors a small group of Latino kids for free," James added.

"Volunteer work. That's really great, very impressive. I made a large donation to a women's shelter in Oakland last year," Jack said.

"I'm impressed," Anya said.

"What does James do?" Jack asked.

"He lives," she said.

"Exactly. He only lives. What does he have to show for that?"

"A life."

"Forgive Jack," James said.

Jack continued, "I didn't mean it in a bad way or anything, but he's been worried about it for as long as I've known him. He was always saying things like, 'What should we do with our lives?' or 'What should we be doing now?' or 'We're wasting our time.' And then, after that, he just sits there and does nothing."

She took James' hand and pulled him towards her until their bodies touched.

Jack continued, "Then there was the other obsession. Mortality!"

"Perhaps, you can fund genetic research with your friend Greg to make immortality possible," she said.

"A good idea for science fiction," Jack said.

"It's already been done, too many times," she replied.

"But really, he is really troubled by this. Maybe, it was because of the patents being around."

"What do you mean?"

"His great-grandfather's phone patents. They're used everywhere. It's like a memorial buried in the world's technology infrastructure."

"Why didn't you become an engineer and invent things, James?" Anya asked.

"I was sick of science and engineering. Sick of it!" James replied.

"One time, his mom took him to an art exhibit and he saw some statues that were hundreds of years old. Remember that trip, James? He decided he wanted to be a sculptor, at least for a while anyway," Jack said.

"So, why didn't you become one?" she asked.

"I tried," James said.

"What happened?" Anya asked.

"I don't want to go into it. It's boring," James replied and he did not go into it, but it was a significant event in his life.

CHAPTER 14

James' interest in art began when he was fifteen. He and his parents toured Italy that summer, travelling from city to city and hotel to hotel, by train, bus, and rented car. They visited museums, cathedrals, chapels, and town squares with fountains depicting Roman mythology, making the myths part of everyday life.

James had no interest in art, or really anything. The tedious tours and endless lectures on ruins, frescoes, fountains, mosaics, and sculptures bored him terribly. Everything changed one day when they visited https://en.wikipedia.org/wiki/Galleria_Borghese Rome and he saw the statue of Apollo and a wood nymph, Daphne. A placard by the statue explained how Cupid had shot golden arrows into Apollo, causing him to fall in love with Daphne and, at the same time, shot leaden arrows into Daphne, making her hate Apollo. Apollo pursued her through the forest, and was about to reach her. She dropped her veil exposing her skin, giving Apollo one tantalizing glimpse as well as a single touch, then she became a tree and her skin turned to bark and Apollo could not express his love for her. The myth broke his heart and he pondered it for days afterwards, imagining Apollo's unrequited love for Daphne. He had romantic fantasies about her the rest of the trip.

The sculptor was a man named Gian Lorenzo Bernini. He created the sculpture in 1622, nearly four hundred years ago. James realized that thousands of patrons view his work each year, and that through the statue, Bernini lived on after his death. It was immortality. Perhaps, an imperfect immortality, *but a lot better than nothing*, he thought

James decided he wanted to achieve this imperfect immortality by making a marble sculpture of himself, his parents, and his pet rat, Alfred, as well as other things that he loved. He imagined each subject and developed an ability to close his eyes and reproduce an image in his mind that was complete and detailed. He could actually rotate it in his head and see it from all angles.

"Mom, how do you become a sculptor?" he asked.

"You need lessons. Would you like to take art lessons?"

His mother enrolled him in an art class that met once a week. A young Russian woman taught the class. Her name was Olga and she had a Masters of Fine Arts degree from the University of Moscow, where she met her husband, who studied Computer Science. They came to Silicon Valley and her husband worked at Google, a company co-founded by another Russian immigrant, Sergey Brin.

She taught drawing. The class was for beginners, and James was the oldest kid in the class by several years. He found himself surrounded by children who were all better than he was, to his embarrassment. He had no hand-eye coordination and could not make the pencil or brush do what he wanted. He lacked the patience or perseverance to improve on it. Sadly, the subjects were stupid and childish, like Elmo from Sesame Street or Santa Claus. He wanted to paint Daphne.

The frustration and humiliation destroyed his interest, and he fought with his mother about continuing until she relented and he quit.

"Besides," he said, "I want to sculpt, not draw."

As they waited to be served at La Mar, Jack asked Anya, "So, when did you start writing?"

"When I was a kid. I never thought about it really, it was just something I did, and then I won a contest in Junior High School. That's when I decided I wanted to be a real writer."

"Why do you do it?" Jack asked.

"If I told you, you would think I'm weird."

"You can't be weirder than my friend James. Try me."

"Okay, I have internal narratives that I tell myself, over and over, so I write them out. Mainly because I like to look at it after I've written it. I read it and re-read it. I'm amused by it. Having people read it is also important, but really secondary to me. James reads what I write."

"She hasn't seriously looked for a publisher or an agent or anything like that yet," James added.

"Have you talked to Ronda Caudill?" Jack asked.

"Ronda Caudill? Why does that name sound familiar?" James said.

"Ronda from high school. She was two years younger, maybe that's why. She's a writer and has a small book publishing company. You should contact her."

"I have a collection of short stories. I wonder if she would publish them."

"She might. I'll email James her contact info. If you guys are interested, I can introduce you to her."

CHAPTER 15

James and Anya drove home after dinner. "What did you think of Jack?" James asked.

"He seems like a very nice person, but kind of lonely."

"He's not that lonely. Always seems to have a girl."

"Does he have a girlfriend now?"

"Not sure… maybe not."

"Who was he with before?"

"Oh… uh, I forget her name. She didn't last long."

"And what about the one before that?"

"Uh, yeah, I don't remember that one, either."

"I think that's why he's lonely. What happened to his eye?"

"In his senior year of college, he got involved with a foreign student from Russia. Gorgeous, brilliant, her name was Leena, but she was the mistress of this Russian Bank Executive, the CEO, who had ties to the Russian Mafia. One thing led to another and the mob tried to kill them both. He lost an eye, dropped out of college and never saw Leena again. Ever since her, no one has lasted very long."

"You're making that up."

"I'm not. That really happened."

They arrived home and went to the living room. "I'm going to watch TV." He sat on the chaise lounge and fiddled with the control, surfing channels, looking for something to watch. When his cell phone pinged, he picked it up. "Hey, Anya, Jack emailed Ronda's contact info and a URL to her publishing site to me. I'll forward it to you."

Her phone pinged when the email arrived. She opened the email, clicked on the URL, and went to Ronda's web site.

"She publishes my genre, all right. She's published thirty books, seven of her own. I'm going to work on my stories." She rushed upstairs to the loft, turned on her iMac, and began to review her work.

She flipped through the titles of short stories that were in various stages of completeness, pausing when she came across the very first story she wrote after meeting James. It was *The Shower of Mortification*. It was about the trauma of being peeped upon in junior high school. Writing *The Shower of Mortification* exorcised one of her primary demons. She wrote it one evening after they had been out and had come back to his place. After making love, she refused to come out from beneath the comforter as usual. By this time, they had been sleeping together for months and he had never seen her undressed.

He pulled at the comforter and she pulled back and it became a tug of war, funny at first, but lasting long enough to become irritating to both of them.

"So, what is it with you?" he asked. "I want to see you. What's the problem?"

She cringed and dug her fingers into the comforter. "No!"

He stopped tugging and let go of the comforter completely.

"It's weird that you don't mind being touched. If fact, you like to be touched and to touch in return. You look at me. What's wrong with letting yourself be seen?"

She didn't know what to say.

"What's the matter?" he said and lay beside her on top of the comforter, encircling her in his arms. "What's wrong?"

She said nothing.

"That's okay… I love you anyway," he said. She knew her modesty was not normal, but she did not know what to do about it and remained silent, inert, frozen.

He stroked her head. "You can tell me how you feel." He pressed his forehead up against hers and looked into her eyes.

She panted short, choppy breaths, but said nothing. After several minutes of silence, she spoke, "I just can't do it."

"Why?"

"I don't want to talk about it." More silence followed until she said, "It was when I was twelve, something happened."

His stomach wrenched itself into an angry fist at the thought of her trauma. "Oh, Anya." He stroked her back through the comforter. "I'm so sorry. It makes me angry that someone hurt you. You don't have to tell me about it if you don't want to, but if you do, I promise never to tell anyone else, and it won't diminish my feelings for you in any way. I want to protect you from things like that. I want you to be happy."

"I can't even think about it. It's so horrible."

He sat up on the chaise lounge and looked at the smoldering fire in the fireplace. "Have you ever seen a therapist?"

"Why would I do that? It's not like I have severe mental problems."

"I've seen them for most of my life. I'm not mentally ill, at least, no one seems to think I am. I think most people who see therapists don't have mental problems at all, they're just working through issues and need someone to talk to about them. That's all. It's normal. So, you have never been to therapy?"

"No."

"Have you ever meditated before?"

"Never."

"I learned how to do it years ago."

"Is it something you learned in therapy?"

"Nope. I actually took a class when I was in college. It works. It helps you relax, clears your mind. Let's try it now and see what happens."

"Okay."

"Here's what you do. Roll over onto your back, place your arms at your sides and have your legs slightly apart."

She repositioned herself.

"Are you comfortable?" he asked.

"Yes."

"Good. First, I want you to focus on your breathing. Notice how uneven it is?" She nodded. "Now, we are going to slow it down, make it calm, easy, and regular. Each breath should be deep, measured, and tranquil. Take a breath in, acknowledge it, and then let it out, pause, and then take in the next."

He mostly stopped talking as they focused on her breathing, breathing himself along with her. "Be aware of your chest, rising and falling" or "Breath in… breath out… breath in… breath out."

She chuckled. "Sounds like yoga speak for housewives."

"Riiiiiiiiiight. Okay. Now, I want you to relax all of the muscles in your body. We'll start with your fingers. Bring your focus to each finger and as you do, notice the tightness in it, and then release the tightness, let your fingers go. If your fingers are clenched or rolled up as though they are holding something, unclench them. Now, let's move to your hands and arms. Notice how the muscles are slightly tensed? Release them, let them drop and lay flat." He waited a minute and then said, "Now, let's focus on your legs." From there, they moved on to each body part, bringing it to mind and then relaxing it: her abdomen, her neck, and her chest.

"Now relax, empty your mind of thoughts, focus on the space just behind your eyes. If a thought appears, erase it and come back to that space. Continue until your mind is blank."

He was quiet for a minute, and then repeated, "Focus on the space just behind your eyes, empty your mind of thoughts. Relax your arms, relax your legs."

She focused on the spot and relaxed her muscles while her mind slowly emptied. He sat by her, patiently, quietly, occasionally reminding her to clear her mind. After a while, the anxiety was gone.

"How are you feeling?" he asked.

She took a slow, deep breath, and while exhaling, said, "Goooooooooooood."

"Do you feel like you can tell me about it now?"

She hesitated.

He said, "You don't have to ever tell me anything about it. Just know that your secret is safe with me and I am angry at whoever did whatever to you."

"It's okay. I want to tell you. This is what happened."

She related the humiliation of the Shower of Mortification in the gym and of the janitor who suddenly appeared, hiding in the closet. She told him that she had dropped her towel, which allowed his hungry eyes to slurp up an unfettered view of her naked innocence and of the humiliating inquisition that followed with her father, principal, and police officer. She felt the janitor held her image hostage and she felt eternal shame about it.

Tears streamed from her eyes, and her voice cracked and she sobbed for minutes at her rage and humiliation over the event. Then she became silent. She felt cleansed and absolved. The tears evaporated from her warm, flushed face.

James was so relieved it was only a Peeping Tom. He understood her trauma was great, but was grateful that she had not suffered through something much worse, like rape or molestation.

"Shhhh, Anya," he comforted her. "I feel your pain." He pulled her into a sitting position, with the comforter carefully wrapped around her as she hid beneath it. He moved his lips to her cheek and kissed her. "It's okay. It was a long time ago. They can never hurt you again. None of them can. Think of it as if it happened in a previous life, separate from the life you live today."

Her dread became relief. She realized that she was safe. Her tears stopped. She dropped the comforter and leaned back on her elbows so that he could see her breasts for the first time. She closed her eyes, turned her head to one side and blushed.

That night she wrote *The Shower of Mortification*.

CHAPTER 16

After writing *The Shower of Mortification*, Anya began a slow surrender towards total nudity. In the beginning, she huddled beneath the comforter, revealing only her face, shoulders, and breasts, while her more intimate parts remained hidden beneath the comforter. Their tug-of-war continued and he gradually gained ground, inch by inch, proceeding towards her navel and then belly, and onwards until she found herself completely nude before him, blushing hues of pink.

He was entranced! He spent hours feasting his eyes on her, standing over her absolutely still for minutes at a time, occasionally turning his head so as to see her from different angles or repositioning himself, shifting his shoulders or bending at the waist, or taking a step to one side or the other, and then standing still to take her in again until each synapse in his mind captured a new image of her.

As he slowly stepped about her, she felt as though he was doing a sort of primitive dance with improvised steps.

He marveled at her sleek skin and rounded contours and at her hair that lay flat on the mattress, rising upward from her shoulders like flames. The minutes stretched into extraordinary hours, during which he was aware of nothing else except his desire to watch her for eternity.

She looked back at him and admired his statuesque physique, his gray eyes, and his face, which reminded her of a hero in a Greek myth; a hero trapped by an eternal pursuit that never resolves, like Sisyphus and his rock, or Narcissus and his reflection, except James was obsessed with Anya instead of himself. She imagined that he was consumed by a desire that he could not quench or express in language or understand in thought, as if it was miraculous and supernatural. The hero spent his life tormented by the riddle of his desire, gazing at her, studying her, encircling her, puzzling out the answer to his own internal mystery, to no avail.

As she grew more at ease, she allowed him to adjust her body, moving her arms overhead or by her sides, looking at her with legs together or slightly splayed. After he positioned her into each pose, he walked about her and observed her. The poses grew more elaborate, some sitting positions, others on hands and knees, or kneeling with hands on thighs or hands hidden behind her back, with her head tilted downward while her long red hair draped forward, hiding the secret of her face. One day, as they lay naked on the chaise lounge before the fire, he produced his SLR camera. "I want to photograph you."

"No." She pulled the comforter over her.

"Come on, Anya. I want to capture you so that we will always have it. They will be for our eyes only."

"How do I know the photos will be kept private?"

"You can trust me."

"No."

"You don't trust me?"

"It's more than just trust. What if you make a mistake and then they find their way onto the internet?"

He understood her concern, but the desire to photograph her nude bedeviled him, and days later, he brought it up again. "We're only young once. Our beauty will fade. I want to capture you now, so that we can have it for the rest of our lives."

"No."

She recalled the other photos he had taken of her and how he had meticulously printed and framed his favorites and had made an album of them. She realized that photography was his only outlet, his only self-expression, and that she was blocking his instincts and impulses. She felt guilty and struggled with his new desire for her. She came up with a compromise. They would keep the camera in a safe that had a combination lock. They would share the combination; she keeping the first three numbers and he the last three.

One night after making love, she retrieved his camera. "I will let you photograph me."

He looked surprised. "What about the photos falling into the wrong hands?"

"I've solved that." She left the room and returned carrying a heart-shaped box with a combination lock. She put it down on the chaise lounge. "Here, we can keep the camera in this. The combo has six numbers. I will set the first three, and you the second three. This way it takes both of us to open it."

He laughed. "That's ingenious. What if we forget the combo?"

"Then the photos will be lost forever."

"What a sad thought. I swear I will never forget these three little numbers as long as I live."

She handed him the camera and lay on her back with her hands over her head. "I am surrendering to you. Do as you please with me and the camera." She closed her eyes, turned her head to the side as she again surrendered to his desire and need.

CHAPTER 17

Posing nude only heightened his obsession with her and created a new frustration, which was a desire to print the nudes, but she would not agree to it, so he buried himself in printing the other photos, the clothed ones of her that captured an endless number of faces expressing mirth, innocence, glee, and nirvana. He experimented with different paper-types, inks, and colors. He had photographed everything he could about her while she read or wrote or spoke or sat, pensively staring into space. He captured her everywhere, in the house and around the city, sitting in sidewalk cafes, or walking in the Marina, or by the Palace of Fine Art, as well as photographing every square inch of her clothed self, including close-ups of her face, her mouth, her eyes, and even just one eye, magnifying the endless fractal of her iris.

Nevertheless, this was not enough, so he printed the photos again and again and then cut them to pieces and glued them back together to make mosaics of her, which he collected together into an album. He placed the album near the chaise lounge so he could grab it whenever he liked and gaze upon the Anya mosaics. Soon, the mosaics lost their novelty and not only bored him, but embarrassed him by how ridiculous they were. He considered throwing them out, but as they were images of her, he could not, so instead he bashfully hid them away.

After losing his desire to print the photos and make mosaics, ennui returned, and with it the slowing of time to the point where he noticed each second tick by; empty, meaningless, irritating him, unsettling him, making him whiffle about the house in search of something, anything. *What, though?*

He had no idea until it slowly dawned on him that he could make little statues of her from paper mache and photos, but then he thought, *What a stupid idea,* and recalled making paper mache in third grade. *What was the recipe again? One part flour, one part water?*

The idea gnawed at him. He began to wonder what it would feel like to make a statue; what it would be like to see it and to have it. He realized that making paper mache statuettes was no worse than making mosaics, and the mosaics had brought him temporary happiness. *And besides, I have nothing else to do, so why not?*

He went to the kitchen, poured a cup of flour into a bowl, added water, gathered together a small pile of photos, and began to work. He crumbled pages of newspaper onto which he applied the mixture and molded it into the form of a standing woman. He dipped photographs in the gooey paper mache and attached them to the shape, slicking them down with water until they lay smooth.

He tried to make the paper mache statue look as exactly like Anya as possible, with her face, chest, hips, arms, and legs all meticulously cut from photos and plastered onto the statue in the right paces. He stood the small statue on the kitchen table and then stepped back to behold what he had made. What he saw pleased him, and he became filled with a kind of euphoria he had never felt before. *This is what I want to do. To make figurines of her,* he thought. The figurines rescued him from ennui. He made several more and then presented them to Anya.

"Look at this, Anya. What do you think of them?"

She recognized his creativity and understood that there was something inside him begging to get out, but she also worried about the euphoria, which seemed slightly manic. She knew his inspired activity would last days and be followed by lows. She worried whether he was normal. She did not want to hurt him, and so she said little about it. Eventually, she decided that the mild mania was not destructive at all and that it brought him enormous happiness, so she decided that instead of being afraid or critical, she should embrace it as part of who James was.

She asked him why it was so important to him to make the statuettes. He did not understand the instincts and impulses that drove him and he had no clear answer for her. For days, he puzzled over it to no avail, until one night he dreamt about it.

In the dream, he led a small tribe of men, women, and children who were all wearing animal skins and hiking through a forest by a river. They were Neolithic people. Their hair and faces were filthy. The men had wild beards. On the other side of the river, broad faced granite cliffs rose vertically for several hundred feet. Large petroglyphs scratched onto the cliffs told him to follow the river, and so they did. Eventually, they rounded a mountaintop and a brilliant cerulean sea came into view. There was a village with hundreds of beige huts with pink tiled roofs extending from the beach up onto surrounding hills.

Suddenly, he was standing in the village square, alone. At the center of the square was a bronze statue of a Greek warrior more than twice his height, crouching, peering over his round shield, ready to strike with a lance. He wore a helmet that had a large crest on top and a bronze faceplate that covered his face. His muscles rippled beneath a leather breastplate. James gawked at it, his mouth hanging open, paralyzed by the feeling one has when experiencing something extraordinary for the very first time.

On the far side of the square was a Greek temple with marble columns capped by scrolling capitals. Behind the columns, he saw the outline of a giant seated female form. Flowers, fruits, and other offerings lay on the steps. Suddenly, he was standing on the steps of the temple. Then he heard a man's voice say in an astonished tone, "The life force is all powerful."

He awoke.

He found himself in the living room on the chaise lounge with Anya, who slept, snoring softly. As he thought about the dream, an epiphany unfolded in his mind. He recalled something he had learned in college.

When James was eighteen, he went off to college to the University of California, Santa Cruz. The university was up in the Santa Cruz Mountains, in a forest of Redwoods that covered the ocean-facing side of the mountain range. The forest stretched from the city of Santa Cruz northward, forty miles to the small town of San Gregorio, which is little more than a gas station and trading post. Three miles west of the campus and hundreds of feet below, was the sea, which creates dense fogs that hydrate the redwoods.

Hidden beneath the dense canopy of redwoods, university buildings sprawled amid trees and ferns. Where there was enough sunlight, clovers the size of half-dollars grew in patches. A thick mat of brown leaves and redwood fronds covered the forest floor, each frond had a central spine with needles attached to it, like the oars of a crew boat.

Having no need for a career, James was free to study whatever he wanted, so he turned to his childhood interest — art — and quickly failed at it as he didn't have the most basic technical skills, like sketching. In spite of his frustration, he lacked the drive to acquire any of the technical skills required of an artist, so he settled on Art History, a major that required studying art and writing papers about it. This made him a voyeur into the world of art. He was a C-plus student.

In an anthropology class, he learned about Venus Figurines, statuettes carved by ancient peoples who lived in European caves around twenty-five thousand years ago. They carved them in mammoth ivory, calcite, limestone, and bone. They are called Venus Figurines because of the subject matter; voluptuous naked women with exaggerated private parts. Their bodies were fat and fleshy, and probably wobbled when they walked. He thought they might represent the ideal female form to a Neolithic artist (if there was such a thing) because fat meant abundance, comfort, and leisure. He imagined a Neolithic man scrapping away at a mammoth tusk or deer antler while a spoiled Neolithic princess, jiggling with fat, playfully posed. Carving figurines took time, time the artist spent focused on his task, taking one scrape at a time, for a time measured in lunar cycles. At eighteen, none of this mattered to James. Instead, he focused on their bodies and their ginormous body parts, primitive and brutish, like Picassos. To James, this by itself was sufficient motivation to make the statuettes.

There was one Venus Figurine that he did not understand: the *Venus of Brassempouy*. It depicted a young woman with braided hair. The statuette was not about her body, but rather about her face — and more than just her face, her state of being, which gazed back at the viewer from twenty-five thousand years ago. The statuette captured the delicate trace of her soul and carried it all these millennia, hibernating in the muddy sanctuary of the cave, until the present.

At twenty-eight, he now understood this. It explained to him why he did what he did. His compulsion to worship Anya came from a primitive drive, a drive embedded in his DNA. It connected him to the Stone Age.

CHAPTER 18

One night, while they lay on the chaise lounge in the living room watching the Late Night Show with Steve Colbert, James asked, "You know those paper mache things I make of you?"

"The statuettes? Yes."

"Yes, well, umm, how do you feel about them?"

"I think they're adorable. I just love them."

"I've made too many, haven't I?"

"Well, how many should you have made?"

"I don't know. It's kind of weird, isn't it?"

"Making little statuettes? Kind of weird?" She smirked because it was kind of weird, but then she added with thoughtful sincerity, "It is a little unusual, but I really don't think it's peculiar or anything like that. It makes you, you. I don't know anyone else who is so engaged in what they are doing. It's a passion, so you have to do it. I think you should make more. I think you should make as many as you can. And... I love them. I think they're beautiful."

With her affirmation, he threw himself into it, happily pouring out his inner self into likenesses of Anya. For James, it was endless pleasure and occasional ecstasy.

Soon, figurines were everywhere: on tables, chairs, bookshelves, and in windowsills. They filled the china hutch and stood in the kitchen and bathrooms. There was even one in the shower visible through the glass door. The living room became a forest of them, so thick that walking between them required care. Still, accidents occurred as they sometimes rubbed up against a figurine, knocking it from its pedestal. It would fall to the floor, or sometimes onto a second statuette, which sometimes fell onto a third. Once, they all fell like dominoes. They looked ghostly at night, lit only by flickering firelight. Eight or so stood like henge stones encircling the chaise lounge that was their love nest, making it into a shrine. Two art deco sphinxes of Anya crouched facing each other at either end of the fireplace mantel, reminiscent of Babylon.

He arranged them and then re-arranged them, photographed them and then printed the photographs. He discovered, for reasons he could not explain, that he made more yellow and green figurines than any other colors. When they discussed them, he referred to them as figurines while Anya preferred calling them statuettes, a word she loved because it rhymed with rosette, which reminded her of pink. This made statuette a feminine word, even though nouns in English lack gender. Anya preferred reds, pinks, and purples to green and yellow and, like James, could not explain why. After she told him this, he began using mainly those colors, not just to please her, but also to please himself by pleasing her. He once secretly tried orange, his favorite color, but it did not work at all, and he kept this one hidden in the attic as though he was ashamed of it.

He had many styles of figurine. Some had correct body parts in the correct places, but most did not. They had themes with photos of Anya in a park or in woods; some had cherubic images of his face with pouty lips, kissing her in various places on her clothed body. There was one photo showing cleavage and another with a nude back that she reluctantly allowed him to use after first disagreeing to it. He longed to create a nude of her, but he knew she would never relent, and rightly so, because to proliferate her nude image in such a manner would cheapen it. Once he realized this, his desire for printing nudes of her disappeared.

He continued, searching for something more, something he, at first, could not define. During these times, he stumbled around, lost, directionless, and depressed until he found a new flavor of figurine which he would then make along with various versions of it, each slightly different. He went on like this until he exhausted all possible permutations, and then he paused.

"I think I've made enough for a while."

During the weeks that followed, they lived among the figurines, awakening to them each day, sitting with them at breakfast, and greeting them in the evening when they returned home after a night out. Anya often read her stories to them before going to bed. To Anya it was art — folk art — and his house a gallery of it.

Every few days one would fall from its pedestal and become dented or torn. Those in the bathroom slowly melted from the humidity of showers and baths. The statuettes in the kitchen became greasy and splattered with bits of food. One in the living room fell into the fireplace and burned while they slept. They discovered the grisly remains in the morning and suffered grief and guilt over their negligence of having placed her so near the fire. They put her ashes in an urn and placed the urn on the mantel between the Sphinxes.

Eventually, the urge to create more returned. "I have more ideas I'd like to try, but…"

"There's no place left to put them," she finished his sentence and laughed.

"Yeah, I know. It's ridiculous, isn't it?" It did seem ridiculous, at least on the surface. He knew he could not stop, so instead he accepted it, chuckling along with her at how ridiculous it was.

She said, "I know what we can do with the statuettes. We can get boxes and put them away. One statuette per box. Chinese lacquered boxes with silk interiors would be perfect." He agreed.

They hiked across town from the marina to Portsmouth Square on Kearny, which is on the cusp of Chinatown beneath the park where Chinese men and woman practiced Tai Chi. They walked past the R & G Lounge, then up Sacramento to Grant and into Chinatown. A clutter of signs with red Chinese characters hung from the gritty buildings. Chinese lanterns dangled from wires overhead. Shop owners peered from their shops from behind parasols made of silk and jade.

Anya and James moved from shop to shop, examining the inventories of boxes, buying one or two here and there until they had thirty or so. Each was different. Some were shiny and black and decorated with scenes of Chinese women dressed in flowing gowns, wearing faces of tranquility and contentment, all made from tiny pieces of mother of pearl. Others were red with dragons in gold leaf. Embroidered silk in orange, red, cyan, and gold lined the interiors.

There were too many for a single cab, so they took two. Once they arrived home, they lugged the boxes into the living room and unpacked them. They solemnly dismantled the shrine of henge statuettes that encircled their love nest, pausing before each and retelling its story, recalling the day the pictures were taken, the theme of the statuette, how they felt that day, mentioning things like 'the misty Redwood forest and ferns' or 'the sand under foot and between toes.' They gently laid each into a box, nestling it into the silk and embroidery and attached a framed photo to each lid so they knew which statuette was in which box.

After the henge was gone, they moved on to the forest of figurines in the living room, saying a few words about each before laying her to rest in a box. Once they had boxed them all, the question became what to do with the boxes?

"How about the garage?" he asked.

"Oh, no. Out in the cold and damp. It will destroy them."

"Yeah, you're right. How about the attic?"

"Alone in the dark? I would feel guilty."

"We can keep the lights on."

She did not like the idea, but there was no other way, so they moved the boxes to the attic. Anya felt so badly about shutting them away that she left the lids open so they could see the outside world, which she knew was a silly impulse, but she gave into it anyway.

James' passion to create returned, and he began to make figurines again, but something had changed. The novelty of the figurines had faded and his inspiration ran dry. It bored him and he even felt a mild revulsion to it, so he stopped cold turkey in the middle of making the first statuette, leaving it incomplete on the kitchen table, malformed like a mutant. He hid it from Anya as he knew she would be upset by it.

He began to see how silly it all was, and the banality of his tawdry craft as well as the fleeting nature of it. *Paper Mache figurines, like third grade art projects*, he thought. He realized the happiness he felt from making the figurines had been a delusion.

In spite of his shame, he missed them terribly, and the house felt empty without them and worse, life had lost its meaning. Instead of being happy in the delusion of the figurines, he became bored and again found himself counting vacuous beats of time as they passed. He pined for the sacred time he had in his delusion, but now that he was aware of it, there was no going back. His dissatisfaction saddened her, as she understood that his drive to express the very force of his life was now gone, as though he had died a little.

Without the delusion of the figurines he was lost, unfocused, and uncentered. He suffered from the persistent torment that always follows euphoria. He paced around the house, trying to shake loose from it, but to no avail. He looked for things to do, picking up magazines, flitting through the pages, each page becoming jumbled nonsense, ungrammatical and unreadable. He turned to the World Wide Web for solace, surfing for hours, finding nothing. Mania destabilized his mind. He felt dizzy. He perspired for no reason. It was purgatory.

His only comfort came from Anya: touching her, holding her, listening to her read. She gladly gave him comfort, reviving him until he slipped back.

Her phone rang. "It's Roger," she said and answered it. Although she had moved in with James, she still kept her room with Roger and Frederick — her surrogate family, so to speak.

"OH, MY GOD," she gasped, startling James.

"What's the matter?" James said with alarm.

"I'm so sorry, Roger," Her voice cracked. James could hear Roger whimpering through the phone, but could not make out a word of it.

"They're putting Norman to sleep tonight. He's dying and in great pain," she explained. Norman, their Pomeranian, was like their child and Roger was beside himself with grief. She said to Roger, "I want to be there with you. I will meet you at the vet. Please, text me the address."

She came into the living room, eyes wet with tears. "I have to go... to see Norman one last time. Roger was crying." She closed her eyes. Tears rolled down her cheeks.

"I'm sorry. Can I give you a lift?"

"That's okay, I'll take Uber."

"When are you coming back?"

"I don't know. I'll call you."

She hurried upstairs, rattled about the bedroom for a few minutes, and then she was gone. Later, she called to say that she would spend the night at Roger's to keep him company while they mourned.

Anya's absence crushed him. Involuntary thoughts raced by, disorganized and in total disarray. He lost control over the small muscles in his legs and abdomen, which twitched and shivered, and kept him from lying quietly to watch a ball game on TV. He tossed and turned until he gave up and left the TV to wander aimlessly through the house, leaving the game on as background noise so that it might cover up the echoing shuffle of his footfalls. He had a chest full of grief over the twin losses: the inspired activity of the figurines and the inspiration of that activity, which was Anya. He was lost. There was nothing for him in this time and space, as though he had no reason for being. He needed her. She defined him and he knew no peace without her. It was like addiction and withdrawal.

Suddenly, he knew what to do. He needed to run, to work himself into a deep sweat, to burn away the toxic turmoil and self-medicate with endorphins. He dashed up the stairs to the bedroom, stripped off his clothes, which he tossed into the hamper, and then rutted about in the underwear drawer until he found his running shorts. From another drawer, he pulled a yellow tee shirt that had 'Sverige' printed across it in blue letters. He put on pale-yellow socks and powder blue running shoes, grabbed his keys, and hustled down the stairs through the front door and out into the cold, damp night.

"Ahhhhhhhhhhhhhhhhh," he said as the fog and drizzle cooled his forehead and temples. He ran towards the Marina, his footfalls splashing in puddles on sidewalks lit by streetlights. Beads of water collected on his brows and trickled across his face.

It was nine in the evening and the city crawled with people. To avoid them, he turned left at Marina Boulevard and headed towards the Golden Gate Bridge. He reached Fort Point in about fifteen minutes where he stopped and looked at the dark currents of the bay beneath the bridge. A collection of logs floated just off shore, some carried by waves up onto the rocks, others occasionally bumping into each other, making a low frequency 'bong' sound. The dark bay-waters dwarfed the logs, which looked like sticks floating down a river. *This is the same spot where Kim Novak fell into the Bay in the Hitchcock film* Vertigo.

He left, running under the Golden Gate onto Lincoln Boulevard heading towards Sea Cliff, a neighborhood of mansions that overlooks the bay. He was mindless in the night, devoting just enough attention to running to avoid tripping or colliding or crossing on a red light. The rest of his mind was devoted to the photos, the figurines, Anya, and the problem of his addiction to her. He was on autopilot, unable to recall where he had been and unable to consciously choose where to go next.

An hour later, he reached Point Lobos where he saw the ruins of the Sutro Baths next to the sea. His mind returned to the present. He stopped to look at the ruins, which seemed timeless in the moon's gray light. Thundering waves crashed onto the beach and became hissing foam that raced up the sand and swallowed it before sliding back into the sea. He and Anya had come here many times and had hiked down to the ruins and walked along the bath wall over the beach. He had taken many photos of her here, some standing on stone pedestals, waves tumbling behind her in the background.

While he stood, his heart beat so hard he could hear it. After an hour of running, he was not tired at all. He decided to run down to the coastline and through Golden Gate Park before returning home. About a mile from home, he stopped and walked. He had run more than fifteen miles in a little less than two hours. His body cooled in the night air as he strolled. Later, he showered and tried to sleep, but his pounding heart and racing mind kept him awake. The run did not work.

CHAPTER 19

Attempts to sleep became futile exercises in laying still, eyes closed, mind racing, jumping from broken thought to thought, not staying long enough on anything to develop it into a theme that spanned more than a few sentences. At around three in the morning, he texted Jack Hooker, 'I can't stand it anymore!!'

Jack's phone pinged, waking him. He rubbed the sleep from his eyes, read the text, and checked the clock. *Jezzus it's early. Must be serious.* He texted back, *'Lee, Lee. What's it all about?'* which did not make any sense at all, at least not on the surface.

James responded, his text shouted with all capital letters, 'PEACE OF MIND!!' The phrase 'peace of mind' came from a morbid experience of Jack's in which he had watched a family member descend into senility over many months. During family gatherings, the man would cry out to his wife, Lee, in a desperate voice that bordered on hysteria, "LEE! LEE! WHAT'S IT ALL ABOUT? WHAT'S IT ALL ABOUT?"

It meant that he had no idea of what was going on and implored the others to explain it to him. Lee mostly ignored him, which cut him off from the world. He could not grasp anything anymore and was now alone because of it. His cry often became a chanting rave, a plea to reconnect to the larger world, but instead of extending him a hand, the others turned away. He begged for solace from the howling winds of Alzheimer's, for peace of mind — a thing he no longer knew — but nothing could be done. It sickened Jack and haunted him for months afterwards. He dealt with the horror of it by turning it into a dark joke: "LEE! LEE! WHAT'S IT ALL ABOUT?" The answer: "PEACE OF MIND."

Since then, whenever life became too much, they would use this phrase. For reasons not understood by Jack or James, the only way to find peace of mind was to do something arduous and mindless in an environment uncomfortable enough to shock their systems and reboot their psychologies. They would deconstruct and then reconstruct themselves anew. It was therapy.

Jack texted, 'Whitney?' as in Mount Whitney, the highest peak in the contiguous forty-eight states at fourteen thousand, five hundred feet. They had climbed Mount Whitney when they were nineteen, completing it in twenty-four hours. 'Door to door', meaning that they left Jacks' place, sped to Lone Pine on the east side of the Sierras, climbed the mountain and drove back to Jack's in less than twenty-four hours; twenty-three hours and forty-two minutes, to be exact. That was almost ten years ago.

'When?'

'Now! Let's go now. Twenty-four hours door to door. It's 3:12 a.m. Pick me up at my place in Moss Beach.' Moss Beach is one of several beach towns along Route One, twenty miles south of San Francisco. It's south of Montara and north of Granada, which is just north of Half Moon Bay. Jack had a bungalow on the cliffs overlooking the sea near Seal Cove, down the street from the Moss Beach Distillery, a restaurant that overlooks the coastline.

'See you then.'

James dashed to his room and changed into jeans, a long sleeve shirt, and boots. He grabbed a parka and went to the garage where he picked up a knapsack, a poncho, a handful of energy bars, four quart-size plastic bottles, and a water pump with a filter. He climbed into the car, checked the time and left. It was 3:16 a.m.

The early morning was a different world. The streets were deserted. It was so quiet he could hear train whistles blow mournfully in the cold night air. He took Divisadero to Marina Boulevard, turned left, and drove between the Palace of Fine Arts and the Saint Francis Yacht club. At Crissy Field, he veered left and found his way to Veteran Boulevard where he headed south. The Boulevard became Nineteenth Avenue and eventually Route 1 as it left the city and headed south towards Pacifica, a small city next to the sea.

After Pacifica, Route 1 narrows to two lanes, and slowly weaves back and forth with a rhythm that relaxed him, allowing his mind to wander back to a strange night he had had in Granada, the small town wedged between Half Moon Bay and Moss Beach.

Was it eight years ago? he wondered. It was. He was only twenty.

On that evening, he and Jack Hooker sauntered into Sam's Chowder House on Route 1 in Half Moon Bay after spending the day hiking on a deserted state beach called San Gregorio. They were sunburned, unshaven, dry, and sandy, their hair made wild by gusts of salty sea wind. They found their way to the bar where they sat on stools. A mirror opposite the bar ran the length of the wall and was lined by bottles of booze. The bartender turned on TVs that hung from the ceiling above the mirror.

They sipped beers and ate clams. From the bar, they could see across the restaurant and out through windows that framed a view of the marina with sailboats slowly rolling in calm water. The sun sank into the sea and it became dark. Nightlife filled the bar with mumbling voices, the clatter of dishes and televisions tuned to sporting events.

The man to James' left paid his tab and began fumbling with his wallet when James heard a woman's voice say, "May I squeeze in between you?" She was speaking to James. In the mirror, he could see a pretty brunette with brown eyes and light complexion and in her early thirties — old compared to James' twenty years. She had long eyelashes and bluish eye shadow. Her thin, pink lips glistened as though wet.

James nodded and she slid her backside up against him while sidling up to the bar. She placed a hand on the stool of the man who was leaving, as if to lay claim to it, and then twisted about to face James, looking into his face with half-closed eyes.

"I'm Lydia."

"James."

Her eyes roamed across his face and then downward while she said to the bartender, "Louis, my usual scotch: a double, neat, and a glass of ice water, please."

"Sure thing, Lydia. How are you doing tonight?" Louis asked.

"I am well, thank you; and you?"

Louis leaned over and quietly said to her, "I'm off in a couple of hours, what are you doing later?"

"That's nice, can I see a menu, Louis," she said, ignoring his question. He looked miffed.

She settled onto the now empty stool next to James.

"What is your usual scotch?" James asked.

She replied with a languid breathlessness, as though sedated, articulating each syllable while grinning. "Bal ven ee," She stared into his face, avoiding his eyes at first, but then looked directly into them for just a moment, darting away flirtatiously.

"Never heard of it."

"It's a port scotch."

"What's a port scotch?"

"Port scotches are aged in port casks, this one for twenty-one years. The port casks sweeten the scotch with port flavor."

That scotch is older than I am! James thought

The bartender poured a double into a snifter and placed it on the bar in front of Lydia.

She held up her glass and turned to James. "Can you smell it?" Her eyes were open and inquisitive, round like brown marbles. Her mouth was crooked, her lips parted, her teeth biting down onto her lower lip with a mysterious desire.

He could smell her sweet scotch and wanted to taste it.

"Sip?" she offered, her mouth now a pout, her head tipped towards him.

He sipped. It burned his tongue, but he liked it. "Bartender! Same here, please," James called and waved. Louis acknowledged the order. Lydia gestured to Louis and said, "And a dozen bay point oysters, please."

James and Lydia spoke about the weather, nearby beaches, and a nude beach Lydia liked to visit while they slurped oysters and sipped scotch.

While James and Lydia chatted, Jack asked the bartender, "Can you put the game on?" referring to the Warriors' game. The Warriors were playing the Grizzlies.

"It's the last game of the regular season," Louis said.

"Curry could make history," Jack said, referring to James Curry, who played for the Warriors.

"What history are you guys talking about?" James asked.

"Most three-point shots in a season," Louis said.

"I think he's at three-ninety-three. What's the record?" Jack asked.

"Don't know," Louis replied.

"I'm not into it. I just don't follow sports. I'm not a good spectator. What about you, Lydia?" James asked.

"I'm not into it, either. I'm a better exhibitionist than spectator, anyway. So, tell me James, if you aren't a spectator, does that make you a willing participant? What exactly are you into?" She giggled nervously while swinging a leg and looking at him from the corners of her eyes.

"I have an open mind."

"We could watch the game at my place. I have some grass. We could get high," she proposed quickly without pausing to take a breath. This caught him off guard. He hesitated and she chuckled at his hesitation. He could not look her in the eye, and instead, stared at her generous cleavage, noticing a freckle and a bead of sweat. She let him look and even adjusted her position to make herself more visible.

She produced a pen, wrote on a napkin, folded it, and slipped it into his hand. "I live across the highway. At the next light north of here, turn left. Here's my address." She then called out to the bartender, "Louis, please put it on my tab." She gathered her things and stood, facing James.

He didn't know what to say. He didn't know what to do. He stood to say goodbye. She shuffled over to him until their bellies touched. She placed her hands on his hips and planted a wet kiss on his mouth. She looked into his eyes and said, "I have to go now. Hope to see you soon."

She left him in a fog: stunned, oblivious, unsteady on his feet. She had molested him, had violated him, but it so deeply warmed his cockles he could not resist. He wiped the saliva from his mouth and then caught the bartender staring at him from across the bar with a forlorn look, as if he was jealous but accepting of the circumstances. He noticed James looking at him and quickly turned away. James wondered what the bartender had seen and what he knew. It made him uncomfortable.

"Dude, wake up." It was Jack speaking. "Are you okay?"

"Uh… yeah… did you see that? That was Lydia. She gave me her address."

"James! You sly dog," Jack crooned and slapped James on the back.

"Can I borrow your car?" Jack slurred while teetering with shock and drunkenness.

"My car? I don't think so. You've been drink'n. You're unsteady on your feet," Jack said, and it was true.

"I'm going over to her place." He held up the napkin like a trophy.

"You're in no condition to drive my car. Get your own car. You're not driving…"

Jack did not complete his sentence because a woman interrupted him by saying, "Is this seat taken?" She pointed to Lydia's vacant stool. She was a pert Latina, neatly dressed, as though she had just come from the office.

"Uh, no, neither is this one. He's just about to leave." Jack pointed to James' stool. "What is your name, beautiful?"

"Vickie."

"Jack."

James said, "I was just leaving. Keys, please?" Jack handed over the keys. The woman took the stool next to Jack. James waved bye and left for the parking lot.

A thick fog had rolled in. It was quiet outside, the only sound being a lonely foghorn somewhere out in the water and an occasional passing car on the highway. Condensation beaded into drops on the cars' hoods and windows. James did not remember much about Jack's car, not even the exact color. *It was dark. It was Japanese.* That was about all he remembered. *Being a little drunk doesn't help.* He pressed a button on the car keys and lights flashed. *There it is.*

He got into the car and then drove out of the lot heading north on Route 1. It was only a mile or so to Capistrano Boulevard where he turned right and then right again on Alhambra Avenue, a frontage road that paralleled the highway.

She is on Alhambra, less than a mile away.

He drove down the unlit avenue through dense fog and felt lost, so he pulled over and called her. "Hi, Lydia."

"Hi, James."

"I'm lost."

"Oh, you're lost, my poor, silly boy. Tell me where you are?"

"I'm on Alhambra."

"You're close. Do you see India Beach restaurant? A neon sign?"

The sign for India Beach floated in the foggy darkness. "I see it."

"I'm right next to it. Do you see the Mini Mart? Pull into the parking lot in the back. I'm upstairs, the second floor over it."

James found it, parked in the back and texted, *'I'm here'.* He left the car and waited in the unlit lot by the windowless backside of the white building near the door. The door opened and she appeared. She wore a crimson silk bathrobe and slippers.

As he approached the doorway, she stepped over to him, moved her head towards his and said, "Do you know how to kiss?"

"Yes, I think so," he replied. She kissed him, cautiously at first, and then with passion, gluing her lips to his, the kiss breaking with a short raspberry.

"Ah huh… you are a good kisser, James."

She took his hand and led him up a narrow staircase. The stairway was clean, utilitarian, but ugly and newly painted light brown with dark brown molding. The carpet matched the walls. They reached the second floor and continued down a hallway to her unit where she had left the door wide open. They entered. She closed and locked the door and led him to the living room. The television was on and tuned to the Warriors' game. The place smelled like dope.

She kicked off her slippers and plopped down on the sofa. "Come, sit." She rolled her head to one side and looked him in the eye while patting her hand on the sofa to show him where to sit. He sat. She put her bare feet in his lap. He laid his arms across her legs, touching her feet with his left hand.

"Want some?" She held up a pipe. He nodded and she passed it to him. There was a lot of pot in the pipe. After a number of deep hits, he handed her the pipe, but she said, "You finish it." So, he did.

"All gone," he said and grinned.

"More?"

"No, thanks." It was already too much. The grass hit him hard and he sank into a stupor. They sat in awkward silence for several minutes while James tried to collect his thoughts.

"Are you watching this?" She gestured at the TV. He shook his head and she turned it off.

He had smoked too much and the scotch, beer, and dehydration made him very uncomfortable. His heart took off, beating hard. He felt so dizzy that he doubted he could walk in a straight line and worried about passing out.

Her place was neat but seedy — cheap furniture and faux artwork, the kind one might find in a cheap motel. The sofa was old, the carpet frayed. It was strange, unfamiliar, and in his present condition, frightening. He was in no shape to drive or even walk, so he could not leave. He was trapped. He froze for an uncomfortably long period of time, and then said, "So, uh, what do you do?"

"Get high. Enjoy life. What about you?"

"You mean that is all you do?"

"Yeah. It keeps me busy. I'm busy enough. I have a boat. I sail it. I party a lot."

She was detached from a normal, productive, and respectable life, but she was seductive. Her aroma filled the air, possessing his senses. She oozed femininity when she spoke, like a coquette; her head rolling back and forth. She was pretty and delicate and vulnerable and so many other things all rolled into one that he could not count them all, and in his present state of mind, he could not even distinguish clearly between them, either.

"What do you do?" she asked.

"I'm still trying to figure that out," James said, as he had no particular direction or ambition either. They had this in common.

"Do you want some advice? Life is so much easier if you just give up!" she said.

"Give up what?"

"Trying. It's soooo much easier to just relax and enjoy."

"Do you work?"

She smiled self-consciously. "No, I'm divorced. I live on the alimony. I had a great big, old, rich sugar-daddy husband. I made him happy and he has been generous with me. That was years ago. I was very young. I'm in his will."

She radiated cinnamon and other spices and he desired her, but he was frozen by dope and unable to act. She sat up and leaned over onto him, bringing her face up to his. "You're very quiet," she whispered, and then ran the back of her hand across his cheek. He froze. More silence followed until she said, "Would you like to see me naked?"

He was shocked and paralyzed. He tried to speak, but could not. He mumbled incoherently, humiliating himself to her amusement. She got up from the couch, walked to the center of the room, slipped out of her silk robe, and stood nude in front of him with her hands on her hips. She turned around so he could see her backside as well. She was beautiful. His heart beat so hard he shook with each beat. She strutted over to him, sat in his lap, and pressed herself up against him.

"Oh, my God," was the last thing he remembered saying.

CHAPTER 20

James continued on Route 1 towards Jack's bungalow in Moss Beach, arriving at 3:55 a.m. He turned off the highway onto Cypress drive and then onto Seal Beach. He parked in the driveway where Jack stood in the darkness with his gear. They threw everything in the car and hit the road.

Once they were back on Route 1, Jack asked, "So, as one leper said to the other, 'What's eating you?'"

"Oh, man… I'm losing my mind."

"Again? I thought you still hadn't found it from the last time you lost it."

"Very funny! Look, I'm really going crazy. I can't sit still. I can't sleep. I'm obsessed."

"With what?"

"With Anya."

"Anya? Don't you already have her? I mean, aren't you with her all the time? So, why the obsession?"

"She's gone right now."

"So she's gone right now. For what? A few hours or something? Can't you wait?"

"She's gone for a day or so."

"'A day or so?' So, from this you're going crazy? Man! You need some help. They have medicine for things like this. You know, like anti-depressants. A little Prozac would do you some good."

"It's not just because she's gone. There's more to it than that."

"Like what?"

"I don't know how to explain it. It's sort of like a mild continuous panic. I feel like I'm being poisoned by little squirts of testosterone being injected into me every few seconds. They make me twitch. And the pressure in my head! It's about to explode."

"Sounds like a migraine combined with anxiety. Take an Advil and a Xanax and call me in the morning. You'll feel better."

"It's not a migraine and there's no physical pain. And what about the twitching?"

"A case of the twitches... so, you have a twitch."

"It is metaphysical pain."

"Metaphysical pain? That's melodramatic, sounds like a case of *saudade*."

"Oh, so now you're going to use one of your *big ten dollar* words. Never heard of it."

"*Saudade*. It's Portuguese. It describes a state of mind, sort of a sadness, a melancholy, a longing for something that cannot be had, at least in part because the object longed for cannot even be known, so even if you were in possession of it, you wouldn't know it."

"Gee, that's profound. That's ridiculous. Here's my comeback to *saudade*. 'It's important to know what you know, as well as what you don't know.'"

"How can you know what you don't know? That sounds stupid."

"Well, whatever. Anyway, *Saudade* is not my problem. There is no name for my problem. It's about having nothing to do, and being reminded of it all the time, like drops of water from a Chinese water torture. Anya fills the emptiness, and now that she is away, I'm in purgatory. There is no rest, no sleep, no peace. I itch, my muscles twitch."

"Sounds like withdrawal."

"That's what it is, withdrawal. Everything in my head is jumbled up, mixed together, all gibberish and nonsense. Like, when I close my eyes I get eyelid movies of all sorts of weird things. One is of a vacation in Italy I had with my parents when I was a teenager."

"Right. You told me about it, a long time ago. The statue of Daphne and Apollo, right?" Jack replied.

"Yeah. How did you remember that?"

"It sticks in my mind. I don't know why."

"Or the *Venus of Brassempouy*," James said.

"That one I don't remember."

"It's an archaeological thing, a statuette carved from mammoth ivory of a living face. It is twenty-five thousand years old," James said, and then changed the subject. "You know, I tried to calm down, to burn off some steam. I ran fifteen miles. It didn't help at all. Then I had this weird dream. It started with me as a little kid. I was with my mom and dad and we were walking through a dark tunnel. They disappeared and I was lost and it was pitch-black. I couldn't see anything. Then there was a light. I walked towards it and came to some stairs. At the top of the stairs was Anya, standing on a pedestal, reaching out to me... trying to speak. Her lips were moving, but I couldn't hear her."

"Bizarre. I think you need a shrink. So, Anya's at the top of the stairs. What happened next?"

James thought aloud as he pieced the dream back together. "I saw her standing there. She was on a pedestal, and she was nude."

"Nude? This is too much information."

"Sorry, man, but I have to tell somebody what happens next."

"Yeah, I know. I can guess what's going to happen next. Do me a favor; don't tell me."

"No, it's not what you think. I became exhausted and couldn't climb the steps and she looked worried. She reached towards me and wanted to help me, but I collapsed on the stairs and died. I was dead."

"Niiiiiice! You are fucking crazy! You need a shrink!"

"I could still see and hear, and then I floated up the stairs."

"Noooo! The dream goes on after you were dead? You floated up the stairs? Give it up, you did not dream that."

"I did, I did dream this. I could float."

"Okay, so you floated up the stairs. Then what happened?"

"She was still there, but she didn't move, like she was frozen, petrified. I could move around her, see her from all angles. I tried to touch her but couldn't. My arms just passed through her like I was made out of air. There was a mirror. I looked at myself, but I wasn't there. I couldn't see myself. I couldn't see my arms. I was not there!"

"Jezzus. You're in bad shape."

"I'm obsessed. I can't sleep. My head's going to explode."

"You're insane."

"It's love madness."

"And withdrawal. You need to climb Whitney."

"Yeah, climb Whitney," James repeated with a monotone voice.

"May I change the subject?" Jack asked.

"Please do."

"So, I have a new name for my brand of pot."

"Oh, god, not more pot business."

"Yeah, the new name is perfect. It's 'Spice', you know, like from *Dune*, that SciFi novel."

"It's all business and money with you, isn't it?"

"With a touch of creativity."

"Choosing Spice as a name for pot is creative?"

"Well, at least I'm not suffering from withdrawal."

"Isn't your obsession with pot an addiction?"

"I don't smoke it. It's not an addiction at all. It's a healthy mental exercise. Something to think about. It's business. It's capitalism."

"Spice. It almost sounds intellectual."

"You know, *Dune* readers are all pot heads anyway. They're a perfect sub-cultural market."

"What is a sub-cultural market?"

Jack shrugged. "Not really sure."

James then asked, "How about *Star Wars* pot?"

"There'd be a huge licensing fee."

"How about Trump pot? He's a public figure. No license fee."

"Right, he'd have me arrested. Anyway, I like Spice, so that's the name. Also, we've just made a breakthrough. We have genetically modified pot. We invented it. My name's on the patent. It's still marijuana, but it has none of the bad side effects like drowsiness. There are no carcinogens, it's better pot... and here's the kicker, these new characteristics of the weed are not inheritable, the seeds the plants produce don't have the new DNA. It requires that the genes be edited, so no one can grow it but us. We own all the patents. We use the CRISPR gene editor method."

James became quiet. He wasn't listening.

"No response. You're in pretty deep over Anya, huh?" Jack asked, but James said nothing. "How would you like to listen to some Kurt Cobain?" Jack plugged his iPod into the car speakers and played, "Come as You Are". He then said, "Think about the pain of Cobain."

"I'm not that bad off."

After leaving Moss Beach, they headed south on Route 1 to Half Moon Bay, where they turned left and drove up and over the Santa Cruz Mountains and then downward into San Mateo and the Bay Area. They crossed the bay on the San Mateo Bridge and connected with Interstate 580, which was traffic free in the early morning. They took Route 120 towards the Sierra Nevada Mountains, crossing California's Central Valley, which is more than a hundred miles of flat, fertile farmland. They passed countless fields, carved into neat rows, some just dirt, others green with vegetation. Their sameness was occasionally broken by signs, huge in size, of Latino farm workers. The entire time, they listened to Kurt Cobain, whose music deepened James' suffering added layers of depression, futility, and hopelessness. He rolled down a window to let in a blast of cool, moist air.

They drove through Yosemite without noticing the sights or stopping. At Lee Vining, they pulled into a gas station for a pit stop, gasoline, and sandwiches.

Dawn arrived and the sky turned pink above the White Mountains, the mountain range east of the Sierras. They headed south on 395 past Tom's Place, the Obsidian Dome, Mammoth Ski Resort, and the town of Bishop, eventually arriving at the small town of Lone Pine. They left Highway 395 for the Whitney Portal Trailhead where they parked at eighty-nine hundred feet. It was around 9:30 a.m. The high altitude took a toll, raising their pulses, making them gasp for extra air.

"To make it on time we have to be back here by 9 pm at the latest."

"Easy."

They threw on their knapsacks, which held only water and energy bars. They locked the car and began jogging up the trail until the thin air made it impossible to continue at that pace, then they slowed to a fast walk. The trail led them through a forest of pine trees, shrubs, and white granite boulders; some as big as houses. As they climbed, the trees and shrubbery thinned out, disappearing completely at around eleven thousand feet. They hiked the seven arduous miles from the trailhead to Consultation Lake, ascending from eighty thousand nine hundred feet to twelve thousand. The air was thin. Their hearts pounded. "My pulse is like one-forty," James said.

They rested and hydrated themselves with lukewarm water that tasted subtly of plastic while chewing energy bars that tasted vile. The next leg of the hike was the ninety-seven switchbacks. The trail rose from twelve thousand feet to over thirteen thousand six hundred, by switching back and forth nearly a hundred times. At the top, the trail joins the Sierra Crest Trail, which runs along the crest of the eastern Sierras. At the crest of the mountains, a line of granite blades rose from a base of tens of feet to mere inches at their peaks, like the protective plates running along the back of a stegosaurus. From the lake, they could follow the trail with their eyes along the crest until it reached Mount Whitney. Thunderheads enveloped Mount Whitney that flashed with lightening for seconds, and then stopped for minutes, only to reignite and flash again. They heard the faint rumbling of thunder. The clouds made an ethereal arena; the rumble of thunder analogous to the roar of a crowd coming from a sports arena.

"See that?" Jack said and pointed at the flashing clouds. "That's where we're going."

"Shit… Seems kind of scary, like the 'Hall of the Mountain King'."

They re-filled their bottles with water from the lake, dropped iodine tablets into each bottle to kill bacteria, and then began the slow climb up the ninety-seven switchbacks to the Sierra Crest Trail.

Snow covered the switchbacks, making them slippery and wet, slowing their progress and exhausting them. At around thirteen-thousand feet, while still switching back and forth, they entered the clouds, which wet them with hovering droplets and teaspoon-size blobs of half-frozen slush. Soon, they were soaked. The occasional rumble of the thunderhead became fainter and less frequent until it stopped completely. James measured his pulse, which galloped by at one hundred sixty beats per minute.

When they reached the Sierra Crest trail, they stopped and rested and ate more of the vile energy bars and iodine flavored water. James' heart rate fell to one hundred and thirty beats per minute, but would go no lower. The thunder and lightning stopped.

"Let's go," Jack said. They got to their feet and followed the Sierra Crest trail, through a complete white-out that limited their visibility to tens of feet. The path rose steadily upward to the summit of Whitney's fourteen thousand, five hundred feet. Once at the summit, they signed the Whitney Summit book and rested. James' rest pulse was one hundred forty beats per minute, nearly twice normal, and it did not seem like it would come down any further. Altitude sickness began to set in. His stomach churned, his heart pounded and his head throbbed.

"I need to get off this mountain. I'm not feeling well," he said.

On their way down, he felt worse. He compulsively measured his pulse, which peaked at one hundred and eighty beats per minute. After short rests, it came down to one-forty, and then he trudged on for a few hundred yards until his vision blurred and pulse reached its maximum again. He continued in this start and stop manner until they reached the ninety-seven switchbacks. Jack seemed unaffected by the altitude.

Once they reached the ninety-seven switchbacks, James fell to his hands and knees and vomited up undigested energy bars. Then it began to rain. He was miserable, but in spite of his suffering, he could not shake his withdrawal from Anya.

The rain passed. He got to his feet and stared down to Consultation Lake, which was thirteen hundred feet below. He didn't think he had enough energy to trudge down the snow-covered switchbacks, but then Jack sat down on the snow and slid all the way back down in mere minutes. James followed. They rested at the lake.

"We're not going to make it in twenty-four hours," Jack said.

"Last time the switchbacks weren't covered with snow. That really slowed us down."

"And you didn't get sick, either. That slowed us down, too."

As they rested, James' altitude sickness faded, but his obsession over Anya persisted. He had not been cured. He began to think there was no cure.

Their strength returned quickly and they began their trek down Whitney Portal Trail, back to the parking lot seven miles away and three thousand feet below Consultation Lake. Once below eleven thousand feet, the trees returned. They came to a side trail that led to a hot spring. Jack stopped and said, "We're making terrible time. We're not going to make it in twenty-four anyway. How about going to the hot spring?" It had been years since their last visit there.

"Yeah, okay. Things are so much easier if you just give up anyway."

"That's positive thinking. Where'd you get that from?"

"It's just something someone said to me once."

"So, do you want to go?" Jack asked again.

"Sure, sounds good. How long has it been since our last visit? Ten years?"

The circuitous trail threaded between granite boulders, pines, and shrubs on the way to the spring. As they approached, they heard laughter and saw steam floating in the air. They peeked from behind shrubbery and saw two women bathing. Flutes of mist rose from their heads. The air smelled of sulfur. One stood. She was stark naked. Then the second stood. She too was nude. Jack looked at James and mouthed the words, *Oh, my God!*

"Oh, it's so nice to cool down," one said as water vapor rose from their bodies and carried their essence into the air.

"What should we do?" Jack whispered. James held his finger to his lips as if to shush him and mouthed, *Nothing. Let them be. Let's watch.*

The sight of the women splashing in the spring surrounded by huge granite boulders and cliffs rising a thousand feet over them nearly straight up struck a primal chord in James. He thought of classical paintings of bathing nymphs. He noticed that the hot spring had changed little since their last visit. The boulders and cliffs were the same as they were ten years before, steadfast in time. Their permanence coupled in his mind with the ephemerality of the bathing nymphs to produce an epiphany that would change everything. *Marble! A statue in marble. It would last forever. That's what I want, a statue of Anya in marble. A nude!*

CHAPTER 21

While Jack drove them home, James contemplated the meaning of a marble statue of Anya. *It will be work of art that venerates our love, chiseled into stone, immutable, immortal. The statue will be a treasure and will stand in museums, participating in the world as art, making others wonder about us and our love for hundreds or thousands of years.*

He imagined that she would move through an archipelago of museums and warehouses over centuries, becoming lost and then rediscovered, resurrected and exhibited, but eventually forgotten about completely, disappearing from the memory of civilization, over which she would triumph by outlasting it, surviving past the extinction of human beings, passing mutely through the ages of the earth, each millions of years long. He imagined that she rode tectonic plates, centimeters a year, for millions of years, eventually submerging into the sea and sinking into the muck at the bottom, invisible to the worms and echinoderms that live there in their sightless universes. The plates would carry her to the bottom of the Mariana trench, the deepest place in the sea, a place where one layer of the earth's crust subsumes another. Anya would sink inward until the Mother Earth drapes her in her mantle, crushing her, melting her, and forming her into minerals hitherto unknown.

He puzzled over the name, Mariana, which brings together 'Anya' with the word Mar, which is Latin for sea, *Mar y Anya*. *How ironic that Venus would rise from the sea and then disappear beneath it in the end.*

He knew that a marble Anya was his destiny. After completing it, his life would resolve and provide a final resolution to the itching question of what to do. Then he could relax.

Persuading Anya to pose nude will be a huge challenge, he thought, and under normal circumstances he would be right, because under normal circumstance what is posing nude all about anyway? *A cheap thrill! A forbidden photograph, hidden away, forgotten about, lost, destroyed. But my circumstances aren't normal at all. I want it in stone, to last forever. Surely, she'll see the logic of it... how it combines ourselves into a single expression that will last eternally.*

Then he realized that she would reject the idea out of hand because of the *Shower of Mortification* and her phobia of being seen undressed. He changed his mind. *I'll have to persuade her. The reasons for the statue are complex. They will take time to sink in. It will take time for her to accept it. I need a strategy.*

The first part of the persuasion came together in his mind. *I'll use Botticelli's* Birth of Venus. *I'll point out how it immortalized both the model and the painter. Even if no one knows who the model really was, her anonymity being her only fig leaf.*

He felt a twinge of empathy as he thought, *Who was she really? She was someone's child and perhaps someone's mother, someone's lover, someone who breathed and laughed and loved and was loved, who suffered and triumphed and in the end died... but who really knows? No one knows, that's who!*

He hoped she had been happy and then thought, *What was happiness in 1485? Life was short, hard, dirty, tragic. Was she poor? Was she hungry? Was she posing as an act of desperation? Was she a prostitute? Was this art or pornography, and was the artist really a pimp? Did she worry about the horrors awaiting her in hell after death because of her sin, something she surely believed in? Did she confess it to priests?*

It seemed possible that she had been exploited and this made him feel guilty, at least for a couple of minutes until he realized, *She lives on in the portrait, beautiful, mythological. Did she realize that her painting would become famous? Isn't that sufficient compensation for her sin?*

The ambiguity troubled him. He considered other famous Venuses like the *Venus of Urbino* and *The Birth of Venus* by Cabanel and, one of his favorites, *In Front of the Mirror* by Carl Larson. *What about those women? What happened to them? Were they coerced by their circumstances or was it a choice they made freely?*

Then he had a strange thought about a movie in which Julie Andrews appears completely nude. *What about Julie Andrews and 'Duet for One'? She wasn't coerced. She had everything, needed nothing. She did it. Why?*

He then questioned his own motives. *Does a man's artistic expression of his desire for a woman degrade the woman he desires? I don't think it's degrading at all, quite the opposite. I think it is veneration.*

He recalled the remarkable gaze of the *Venus of Brassempouy* carved from a mammoth tusk twenty-five thousand years ago that now looks into our faces as though she is still alive. The artist that carved it was driven by the same passions that drove the other Venus paintings and the same thing that drove James.

So, it's perfectly normal... perhaps, a little obsessive, but I'm well within a range of normal — on the spectrum, as they say.

The normalcy of his desire coupled with his need to venerate Anya made it okay. Having resolved this little struggle, he was free to pursue his destiny without any guilt. His intentions were pure.

CHAPTER 22

Hours later, James pulled into the garage at his home in the Marina. It was 10:30 a.m. He missed the twenty-four hour goal by seven hours but did not care at all. He collapsed on the chaise lounge in the living room. Having not slept for nearly two days and having the trip to Mount Whitney totally exhaust him, he was finally able to fall into a fitful, broken sleep, filled with stressful dream fragments that did not make sense. In one, he had dragged a huge marble boulder up the ninety-seven switchbacks of the Whitney Portal Trail. As he reached the top he realized that the boulder was granite and not marble. He was shocked. *How did I miss that? Does this mean I'll have to drag it back to the bottom?* The thought panicked him. He fell to his hands and knees and threw up. While on his hands and knees, leather hiking boots appeared in his field of vision. He looked up. It was a park ranger. The ranger wrote a citation and handed it to James. It cited him for being 'a blind fool, instead of a blind artist'.

Huh? He was confused. "What does this mean?" he asked the ranger.

"Look," the ranger said and pointed and the cliffs. James looked and saw a gigantic statue of a king sitting on a throne chiseled into the rock.

It was over a thousand feet tall. A crown of lightening flashed about his head. The ranger said, "There, look at it. A monument to a great man."

The sight of the statue filled him with awe. The ranger then added, "Someday, you'll realize that you have wasted your life... and then you will die."

James knew it was true. Even though the end of his life was decades away, he knew now that his life was wasted, meaningless, and worthless. He wept, paralyzed by grief. *Why go on? What's the point?*

The ranger then said, "Put the rock back where you found it," and hiked down the mountain, arriving at the bottom almost immediately. He disappeared.

James nudged the stone but it did not budge. He nudged it again, this time with all his strength. The stone slowly rolled forward and stopped. He pushed it again, and this time it rolled away from him, down the steep mountain on its own, out of control. It accelerated and careened down the mountain, jumped into the air, crashed downward, and then jumped up into the air again. It approached the freeway that appeared at the bottom of the mountain. James realized that the boulder would destroy cars and kill people and that it would be all his fault. His heart nearly stopped. He bought his hands to his head and gasped in horror. Then the freeway transformed into a pond, the cars became orange Koi fish and the stone disappeared. He saw his face reflected in the pond. The fish made ripples on the surface. His reflection faded away and he saw Anya. He felt relief and happiness. Then he awoke. He was alone. The fire had gone out. It was cold.

By midday, he gave up trying to sleep and connected to the internet. He reviewed works of art while trying to decide how Anya should pose.

Soon, he had hundreds of images. He printed them and put them in a loose-leaf folder. Anya came home in the early evening with Chinese food from the R & J Lounge in Chinatown.

They sat on the Chaise Lounge with chopsticks, eating the food directly from the take-out containers. James asked, "How's Roger doing?"

"Better. Still grieving, though. We're going to look for a new dog tomorrow."

"A new dog already? That was fast."

"It's the best way to get over the loss."

"What about Frederick?"

"I don't know. He was away at a conference. I think in Atlanta. What about you? What did you do while I was gone?"

"I was crazy without you here, so I called Jack and we climbed Mount Whitney."

"Just like that?"

"Yep, just like that. I needed it. I was a wreck. I'm better now."

Later that night while they lay on the chaise lounge, he decided to put the first step of his plan in motion. He asked, "Which movie do you want to watch?" He showed her Walt Disney's *Mary Poppins*, a favorite of her childhood. *Mary Poppins* was a book that captured her imagination as a child. She read and re-read it and watched the movie hundreds of times, memorizing melodies and lyrics. *Mary Poppins* brought order and happiness to the Banks family by leading them on a journey of self-discovery. She was like a family therapist. Pert and proper, she was a role model.

"Or would you like to watch this?" He presented the second movie called *Duet for One.*

"I've never seen it." she said and chose it.

Duet for One is a tragic film starring Julie Andrews who plays a famous, classical violinist named Stephanie Anderson. The character discovers she has multiple-sclerosis at the beginning of the movie and then slowly loses her gift to play. As the disease progresses, she loses her ability to walk and becomes confined to a wheelchair. Her husband leaves her for another woman and she eventually dies alone.

Near the end of the film, after her husband leaves, a carpenter comes to work in her home and she starts an affair with him. In this part of the movie, Julie Andrews appears completely naked. She is beautiful! Both James and Anya marveled over Ms. Andrews, who seemed like a goddess. They were mesmerized.

After the movie, James says, "So… look what happened to Mary Poppins."

"I am shocked."

"Beautiful, isn't she?"

"But why would she do it? She had everything, wealth, fame. What did she get out of this?"

"I have no idea."

"I can't believe it. I am so surprised."

"I think she did it so later she would remember what she looked like."

"But why publicly?"

"She has nothing to be ashamed of."

"No… she doesn't," Anya said.

"You have to admit, it is kind of a turn on. She pretends to make love to that guy while being filmed," James said with his devilish voice.

"And then she gives him her priceless Stradivarius, as though she exchanged her musical talent for one last love before the end of her life," Anya added with a romantic voice.

"Did she degrade herself in this film?"

"Well, she did reveal something very private."

"She did, but what was the harm?"

"Nothing."

"I agree. And now she will be able to look back and see herself and how beautiful she was, perhaps when she is eighty or ninety."

"It is a little kinky," she said.

"That's my favorite part," he said.

"Stop that," she scolded.

He rolled towards her and kissed her forehead. "You know I am in love with you."

"Yes, I know."

They spent the next several hours making love, after which, they frolicked about the house naked, showering, eating, resting, and then making love again, so engrossed in each other that they knew not whether it was day or night.

Later, while they lay on the chaise lounge watching the news, he asked, "Do you think too much love can be a sickness?"

"Like if you develop a dependency on it?"

"Like an addiction?"

"Yeah."

"I'm already there. There's nothing we can do about that."

"Let's face it, you're addicted to love."

"I had withdrawal when you were gone."

"Get out of town, you boob. So silly of you." She looked amused.

"I'm serious. I couldn't sleep. I couldn't sit still. I twitched. My muscles spasmed."

Now she looked concerned. "Don't say bizarre things like that."

"I am powerless in the face of it. Why struggle against it? Surrender to it and enjoy it. It's much easier," he said.

She rolled over to him and lay up against his side. "This is what I think, James. I think that the laws of physics and the other basic forces of the universe brought us together, co-mingling our biochemistries."

"That's very clinical, Anya."

"It's so simple, though. It's a chemical reaction: my chemistry reacting with your chemistry, while yours reacts with mine. It attracts us to each other, brings us together, which increases the reaction until we exhaust ourselves, burning up all the chemistry."

"So, you're saying our attraction can't be helped because it is at a molecular level."

"Exactly! We were programmed this way. It is our destiny. You see, the fault lies in our molecules," she said.

"And because it's our destiny, we have no choice and should not feel constrained or guilty in any way about it or what we might do to express it."

"So true."

"Let me show you something," he said. He brought up the internet on the TV over the fireplace and surfed to an image of the marble statue, *Apollo and Daphne*, by Gian Lorenzo Bernini — the same statue that had captured his imagination as teenager in Italy while on tour with his parents. "Look at this. They keep it in the Villa Borghese."

"What is Villa Borghese?"

"Sort of like a museum in Italy. The statue is five hundred years old.

It's Apollo pursuing a nymph in the forest. Her name is Daphne. She doesn't want to be taken by Apollo. She wants, instead, to stay in the forest. Her father is the god of the forest. He turns her into a tree to escape Apollo."

"So, she becomes part of the forest," she said.

"Yep."

"It's about chastity. You can't have relations with a tree. Do trees even have a gender?"

"I think it's about unrequited love and Apollo's eternal longing."

They both paused for a moment while she pondered Apollo's unrequited love and he, the sex life of a tree. Then he said, "I have more I want to show you," and hurried out of the room, returning moments later with the folder of images he had collected and printed earlier that day. He thumped down next to her on the chaise lounge and cradled the folder. She scooted over to him and sat cross-legged, resting her cheek on his shoulder.

The first image was of the *Venus of Brassempouy*, the statuette carved from a mammoth tusk by a cave person. It captured the face of a young woman who looks directly into the eye of the viewer from across a chasm of time twenty-five thousand years wide.

"The person who made this loved her," he said. "It is a testament of this love and it has survived for twenty-five thousand years in mud at the bottom of a cave. It was re-discovered around fifty years ago. Someone tossed the statuette into a cave, thousands of years ago, giving it to Mother Earth to protect and nurture, like a seed." He paused to let what he had said sink in, and then continued, "These are all Venuses, all inspired the same way, by the same thing, which was love." He showed her image after image of painted Venuses, sculpted Venuses from the renaissance and romantic eras, and also Venus Figurines from the Neolithic, all intermixed with images of Anya, clothed, because he would not print the nude images of her.

Her pulse quickened as she sensed that something new was afoot, a desire to start a new project, a new obsession. She felt both excitement and dread. Whatever this new thing was, it had cured his depression. He was calm. He was centered. He seemed happy. *But what will he ask of me this time?*

She braced herself for what he would propose next. She knew that she would struggle to accept this new thing, at least in the beginning. But then the fear and anxiety would fade, and she would agree to it, and probably discover that she enjoyed it and would add to and embellish it herself, making a fetish of it, as well as writing about it as their love inspired many of the stories she wrote, all in the tawdry genre of romance.

He showed her Venus Paintings, like *Venus with a Mirror*, Cabanel's *Venus*, *Venus de Urbino*, Larson's *Before the Mirror*, Bougereau's *Birth of Venus*, Manet's *Olympia*, the *Venus of Boucher's*, *The toilet of Venus*, *Venus with Organist*, and *Cupid* plus the archeological Venus Figurines of Willendorf, Lespugue, Brassempouy, and others.

"All of these are nudes," she said.

"They are."

"We've had several conversations about this, already, haven't we? Even on our first date we did, remember, in the gift store at the De Young?" She reminded him of the posters at the gift shop in Golden Gate Park and the poster of *Before the Mirror*, and the delicate nude woman who seemed to wilt with fatigue while a lecherously, leering older man, who was dressed to the nines, wealthy and powerful, ruling over her, tried to paint her. She understood that the man was at the woman's mercy, because his desire for her controlled him. The artist took her in to himself and then poured her out onto canvas with paint, trying to capture the elusive kernel of their love. He was never satisfied.

"Yes, I know what you mean, except this is different," he said.

"I don't see how it can be any different."

"You haven't heard me out yet."

"I am not going to allow you to print nude images of me, if that's where this is going."

"That's not exactly what I had in mind."

"Really? Well, I'm not sure I even want to know what you have in mind."

"Well, I was thinking of, uh, like..." he said, and then paused.

She held her breath in anticipation, and then said, "Yes?"

"Well, like a figurine."

"You mean statuette?"

"Yes, a statuette."

"You've made them before."

"This is different."

"How?"

"Well, it will be a lot bigger. Umm, like, life size."

She paused, rocked her head to one side, and said, "A life size statue of me. What kind of scene? What would the background be?"

"What kind of background? You mean like, where would you pose? Hmmm, let's see. We should talk about that. Where should you be? Where would you like it to be?"

"I have no idea. I need to give that some thought," she said. "You probably like the idea of a forest and nymphet."

"The 'where' of the statue is really not that important. What matters is the foreground, the statue — by that, I mean you — so the background would be abstract and timeless."

"What would I wear?" she asked.

"Well, Anya, the problem is that clothing is not timeless."

"So, what does that mean?"

"Clothing would not be part of the statue, is what that means," he said.

"You mean a nude?"

"Yes, a nude."

"Have you lost your mind?" Now she was afraid. This was how each little journey had begun before: a proposal, her shock over it, his persistence, and then finally her surrender to it. Her willing, if not enthusiastic, participation always followed.

"This is the cure and it will end my obsession and my suffering over it."

She was silent.

"If I am crazy, I am not the first one to be crazy like this. Look at the work. It is for the love of women. I need to do this. I need to express my love."

She saw the logic of it and she felt his passion, but she could not surrender to it. *Even if Julie Andrews did,* she thought. She said, "I'm not doing it."

"Why not?"

"Well, let's start with other people seeing the statue. I mean, Jeezus."

"Well, we could hide it."

"That doesn't make any sense."

"No, really, I have it all planned. In the attic. Let's build a tiny room with a locked door — with a combo lock, kind of like the camera we keep in the heart-shaped box. We can place it on a pedestal. Only you and I will be able to go into the room. The figurines could keep it company."

"Don't be ridiculous. And have you thought about after we die?"

"I have. It is a romantic idea, don't you think? 'The afterlife of the statue'. You could write a story about it; the totem of our love. How we pass on and then the secret behind the locked door is finally revealed; a statue of Anya surrounded by paper mache figurines."

"Forget it, James!"

"You know, you're cute when you're angry."

"THAT'S NOT FUNNY!" She stormed out of the room.

James was undeterred and brought it up again a few days later. "Have you given the statue any further thought?"

"No, not that again." She shook her head. "James, it is so ridiculous. I mean, how can you really… What are you going to do, learn to sculpt in marble? How long will that take? Ten years? Is that something you really want to spend all your time doing?"

"Oh, no. I can't do it myself. I could never create what I have in mind. I want a work of art, a great work, something classical, something that would last through for centuries, like Apollo and Daphne. I could never achieve that. I want to hire a sculptor. I'll commission the work."

"You'll hire someone to make it?"

"Yes."

"So, I will pose for them naked?"

"Nude, think of Botticelli."

"So, the sculpture won't even be from you?"

He shrugged. "The conception of it is from me — and you — this is something we will do together."

"I don't think so. I won't do it."

"Is this because of the *Shower of Mortification*?"

"No. I'm just not going to do it."

"But I need this. I need it to complete my life."

"Melodrama and emotional blackmail, really? To 'complete your life'? You must think I'm a fool."

"I'm sincere. You've seen how I suffer. Think of the *Venus of Brassempouy*. I want to make the same of you; I want a statue of you in marble that will be kept and preserved until the end of mankind and civilization, and millions of years afterward."

She had seen him suffer and she knew he was sincere and there were aspects of his proposal that she liked, but she could not break through the terror of being seen nude, so she made him a promise. "Okay, I'll do it, but the sculptor can never see me nude."

"How about a reflection of you? Or a photograph?"

"No... I'm sorry, James. I just cannot be seen."

CHAPTER 23

James was at a loss. He understood the depth of her phobia at posing nude and knew there was no way around it. Her trauma blocked him from completing his life. However, his obsession over it persisted. He recalled the nude bathing women surrounded by the permanent rocks and cliffs of the Sierra Mountains and the unsettling dreams about wasting his life, which only convinced him further that he needed the statue of her, but there was no solution. Her phobia stopped him from completing his destiny.

He decided to distract himself by photographing The Fool, the guitar he and Anya had purchased at an auction months before. He kept The Fool in the living room, near the chaise lounge, all this time. That night, he carried it to the studio, found a stand with a saddle into which he carefully placed it. He then turned on the archaic stereo that his parents had purchased decades ago. The CD carousal spun and selected, at random, a song that he recognized. The song was old, from the 1960s, one his parents listened to when he was very young, called *Spill the Wine*. It brought to mind a hippy dinner party with a Late Sixties theme, held by his parents, here at this house in the Marina. Participants dressed in Tie-Dye shirts and bell-bottom jeans. Some of the men had beards and shoulder length hair. The air carried the odor of marijuana surreptitiously smoked on the balcony and nostalgia for anti-establishment themes and protests, nearly all of which had evaporated from American Culture.

As he rocked to the music, he got cameras, lenses, and filters and placed them on the desk near the guitar. He positioned lights and cameras and commenced photographing. After a few minutes, he stopped and examined his work. He was dissatisfied with it. He sighed and looked at The Fool. It inspired nothing in him. Instead, thoughts of a marble statue of Anya invaded his mind. The guitar was no substitute for the statue.

He decided to go out for coffee at Cumaica, an artisan coffee shop on California Avenue, a short walk from his home. He ordered a double espresso and bought a San Francisco weekly. He sat outside on the sidewalk in the morning sun, stirring his coffee, scanning the tabloid, trying to evade his thoughts on the statue. He noticed an article about a blind sculptor.

A blind sculptor? How can this be? He read on. The article told Feo's sad story, about how he had lost his sight as a child and had learned how to make Day of the Dead figurines and how he had sold them to churches in the inner city of Los Angeles in the beginning. Now, he was an up and coming artist in San Francisco.

After going blind, Feo's parents took him to *La Iglesia de Nuestra Señora la Reina de los Ángeles*, a Catholic church founded in 1784, near Olvera Street and Union Station in downtown Los Angeles. It is an active and vibrant Catholic Church, holding weekly mass and celebrating most Catholic holidays, including Christmas, Easter, Ash Wednesday, Palm Sunday, and All Saints Day, which is also known as the Day of the Dead. Services are attended primarily by Latino immigrants from

Mexico, Guatemala, El Salvador, and Honduras.

The priests took pity on Feo. They gave him menial jobs and a few dollars a day — money his family needed. A blind priest, Father Phillip, took Feo under his wing. He taught Feo how to read Braille, how to find his way in his new blind world, and the art of self-defense so he could protect himself against those who might prey on him. Feo assisted the priests with the many holidays celebrated each year and became an expert on the rites and rituals of Catholicism.

During the Day of the Dead celebration, Feo took clay and fashioned it into a skeleton figurine of a man with a Sombrero. Father Phillip praised his work and encouraged him to make more, which he did, and soon he had many. The priests used the figurines in Sunday school art projects where children painted them with bright colors. They called them *Los Muertos*, which means 'the dead' in Spanish. Word of his figurines spread, and soon he received requests from other churches. He began to sell them; fifty a week. Because he could not see, painting the figurines was impossible, so he instead focused on their form, sometimes using toothpicks held between teeth, which gave him more sensitivity and control and increased the resolution of his detail.

"They are masterpieces," a sighted priest commented. Another said that God had given Feo a gift to replace his lost sight. Feo threw himself into *Los Muertos,* becoming a factory of figurines, all for the Day of the Dead — happy skeletons of men with mustaches, women, children, a mariachi band, dogs and donkeys with sombreros, skeletons riding donkeys, a family of happy skeletons.

He won a scholarship to a small art school in Los Angeles when he was fifteen. Later, he attended art school in San Francisco. He was still relatively unknown. He worked with clay and stone, including onyx, obsidian, and marble. He had branched away from Day of the Dead themes and moved on to still life, including nudes of women.

The root of Feo's art is in death, darkness, and the loss of sight. Poor fellow! James thought, and considered himself lucky to have never known a terrible loss like that. He brought up Feo's website on his phone and dialed the number on the site. An answering machine picked up and a woman's voice said, "Please leave your name and phone number and we will call you." He hung up.

But can Feo make inspired art? Can he make the treasure I want? James wondered, and then thought, *Do I really* want *to hire an artist whose artistic force comes from death? It would be like making a deal with death.* The thought struck him as ironic. He wanted to make a work of art about love, something that drives the creation of life. Could he use Feo, whose inspiration came from death? The idea amused him, but did not stop him. He soon forgot about it.

The address of the workshop was on the website. It was south of Market near Third and Bryant. He left the café and hailed a cab. Fifteen minutes later, he arrived in Feo's neighborhood of auto repair shops, warehouses, and parking garages. He knocked on the door. There was nothing. He knocked again. Then, from behind the door, a male voice with a Mexican accent asked, "What do you want?"

"I read about you in *San Francisco Weekly*. I wonder if we could talk."

"What about?"

"Sculpture."

"That is a very broad topic, my friend. We could speak about it for the rest of our lives and still not know what we are talking about."

"I want to discuss a commissioned work."

"What is your name?"

"James Brighton."

The door opened and James saw Feo. He had shoulder length black hair pulled back into a ponytail. He had a brown pockmarked face. He wore dark glasses, blue jeans, a faded red tee shirt with the words, '*Los Aztecas*'.

"I am Feo, please come in." James followed Feo into the center of the workshop. "Have a seat, my friend." James sat on a white love seat.

The studio was filled with statues made from different types of stone and many different colors: translucent whites, greens, reddish-browns. Most were of people. There was a headless man, naked and walking, tender statues of graceful women and Minotaurs of different sizes and colors. There were Mexican themes, one of a Mariachi musician playing the trumpet, wearing a broad sombrero and ornate outfit, another was of a child kicking a soccer ball, another a mustached Mexican man holding a rooster firmly in his hand. There were religious themes: a procession of priests, one swinging a thurible to clear their path of spirits; a priest speaking from a pulpit, arms held outward, eyes closed as though reciting a prayer; the face of Jesus whose message saved Feo from poverty, deprivation, and perhaps death.

And there was an abstract statue, a pile of breasts, some black, others shades of brown, and many translucent white, all with different colored stone for their nipples. James immediately recognized Feo's talent. He knew Feo was the man.

"How can I help you?" Feo asked

He began telling Feo about his problem, his love madness, and his desire to preserve it for all time. He told him how he and Anya had met, about photographing her, printing the photos, the mosaics and figurines, his dissatisfaction, and his need for a true work of art.

Feo sat quietly and listened.

James went on, "I want a nude of her, very detailed, capturing the very force of her life in marble."

"Capturing a life in a work of art is not a small undertaking, my friend. It will be costly. It will take time."

"How much? How long?"

"It is hard to buy what you want. You cannot hurry such things. They gestate in their own time. I will think about it. They require inspiration. You must choose a pose. I need to understand her personality, to hear her voice, to speak with her about it."

James nodded. He understood what Feo meant by 'gestation'. He went through a similar process when it came to photographing guitars.

Feo continued, "And then there is the question I must ask you."

"Okay. What?"

"Are you sure you feel comfortable with another man touching your woman?"

James hesitated, cocking his head to one side, but then impulsively replied, "What do you mean by that? You're going to touch her to produce a commissioned work of art, right? This isn't some kinky, sexual ritual. This is about art and love."

"Well, you might be surprised by some of the reactions I get, but if you feel comfortable, we can proceed."

"I'm okay with it."

"What about her?"

"I'll discuss it with her. After that, what is the next step?"

"The next step is that I meet Anya."

Later that evening as Anya and James relaxed on the chaise lounge, he brought it up again. "Anya, I think I've solved it."

"Solved what?"

"The statue issue."

"What issue? There's no issue. It's impossible. I refuse to be seen naked."

"You mean nude."

"What difference does that make; naked, nude?"

"It's the wrong 'term of art'. I want a nude statue, not a naked statue."

"It's impossible, because the sculptor will have to see me."

"There's another way."

"How?"

"A blind sculptor."

"That's ridiculous. How can a blind sculptor make anything… unless he touches me?" She stopped while the reality of his proposal sank in. "You mean he would touch me. VERY FUNNY!"

He sat quietly and waited.

"You really mean that, don't you!" she said with disbelief. "No, I can't, I can't do it. Don't make me do this, James. I know I said that I would pose if the sculptor couldn't see me, but please, don't make me do this."

"I would never force you to do anything, Anya."

"Does this mean that you won't mind another man touching my body?" she said as a tear rolled down her cheek.

In his enthusiasm at finding Feo, he had not thought through the implications of Feo touching her. The thought of her being touched by Feo suddenly seized him with pangs of dread. Beads of sweat formed on his forehead. He felt clammy, nauseous, and light headed, as though he was going to faint. "I guess I didn't think about that," he said, and then laid down on the chaise lounge and elevated his feet on pillows so the blood would run to his head.

What am I doing? Why am I forcing her to do this? What does this mean to Anya? How does it hurt her? His ineptitude caused her pain. Because he could not sculpt Anya, he needed Feo to create his life's work, and this made him, impotent and a failure. He felt like shit over, but there was no other way.

Anya shivered at the thought of a stranger laying his hands on her. "I can't do it. I don't think I can do it."

"You're right. How can I ask this of you? Let's forget about it."

She tried to forget about it, but thoughts about posing nude and being touched and whether she wanted a work of art of herself continued to bother her. The more she thought about it, the more she found things she liked about it, one of which was the very idea that a replication of her form would be captured in stone and would last centuries, far beyond the end of her life. She began to think, *If the secret of my statue is managed properly, there won't be any shame or embarrassment.*

She dreamt about it. In the dream, she sat in the living room on the chaise lounge, and there was a blind man and she was naked before him. He knew she was nude, but could in no way sense her or perceive her nudity. She felt lustful, but she did not know why. Suddenly, James appeared. He stared at her with a remote, detached look.

"See how she blushes?"

"I cannot see," the blind man replied.

The blind man reached for her, hands open, fingers apart. She closed her eyes and turned away as his hands stroked her soft flesh. An unbearable pleasure caressed at her viscera. She awoke. She felt guilty as though she had been unfaithful to James and kept the dream to herself.

James could not relax. The thought of her being touched by Feo enraged him with jealousy while at the same time the desire for the statue became a craving. It tore him in half. Each time he thought of her being touched, his glands released a flood of fight chemistry that made his heart pound and muscles twitch, after which he would be unable to sit still and focus on anything else. To cope, he went for long runs several times a day, and although this kept him from exploding, he suffered as his heart pounded all day long and his thoughts raced by, mere fragmentary wisps, incomplete and ungrammatical. He could not settle down and lay quietly. Whenever he tried, he twitched and shivered. It was madness.

She saw his suffering and felt sorry. She knew emotional suffering well because of the Shower of Mortification and empathized with him. He had cured her from it, and she felt a certain obligation to him. The sight of his suffering hurt her.

His mania continued into the night, keeping him awake. He could not lay still and fitfully shifted position beneath the covers, laying still for seconds and then shifting. A plague of itches swarmed across his skin like stinging ants, making him scratch and twitch and reposition his arms from beneath the blankets to above because they were too warm, only to have them become too cold, so he would then move them back to beneath the covers, until they again became too warm again.

He went for run after run, sometimes in the small hours of the early morning, running through foggy, deserted streets. He found previously unknown nooks and crannies in the city: tiny patches of grass, private gardens, tunnels, walkways, wooden steps, and alleys, some no more than gaps between old buildings. It was only then that he felt at peace, so he ran and ran and ran without effort, semiconscious, often so deep in thought that the path of his run would become a 'random walk' until he came to dead ends that required he leave his thoughts and return to the present just long enough to understand his whereabouts and chart a new course, that would soon be forgotten. He ran until he was exhausted, and then walked until his strength returned and then he would run home.

Madness possessed him and took him away from Anya, leaving her alone. James was her best friend and lover and the only person with whom she could share her intimate self, but more importantly, he was her muse and his absence left a void in the world of her art. She stopped writing, her creativity wilted, and she found herself with nothing left to think about except the ordinary events of each day: bathing, brushing teeth, cooking, washing — things the internal organs of her mind managed mostly unconsciously. Now, they were all she had. She realized she had to do something about it.

She summarized her feelings about the statue and wrote them out as a list.

1. The immortality of the statue appeals to me.

2. If no one I know sees the statue, then what is the embarrassment, really?

3. Can the secret of the statue be kept? Yes, I think so.

4. James is suffering. I want to cure him.

5. But most of all, I have lost my muse and I want him back. The statue will bring him out of his mood and back to me.

She rationalized the indignity of posing nude and knew intellectually that women and men pose nude all the time, for reasons as unimportant as posing for art students so they can learn to sketch the human form. She realized that while posing and being sketched, their bodies became faceless objects, or mere body parts as a student sketches a hand or a foot, and another, the entire body, blurred and undefined. *What are the consequences for them? I think I could survive posing for Feo.* She knew posing and being touched by Feo would not degrade her in James' eyes or diminish his love and respect for her in anyway. *It will be unpleasant, but I can do it. How will it be unpleasant for him?* She realized he would be terribly jealous, but was not sympathetic. *His jealousy will be the price he pays, just as I will suffer the indignity of posing and being touched. We will survive it, we will remain intact, but we will both suffer.*

James, who had been out for yet another run, appeared in the living room, steaming and sweaty.

"Hi, love," she called to him from the loft.

"Hey."

"How was run? Where'd you go?"

"I ended up in your neighborhood, Twin Peaks. Then I ran home. I need a shower." He walked from the living room, passed the kitchen to the downstairs bathroom, where he turned on the shower faucets, adjusted them to a cool temperature, stripped, and tossed his clothes into the hamper. He tested the water again and then stepped in. He soaped himself, head to toe and then rinsed. He grabbed the shampoo, twisted off the top and was about to wash his hair when the shower door opened. He turned and saw Anya, nude, looking at him in the eye, head tilted, lips pursed, flirtatious and smirking.

"Hey, sailor, how about a date?" She felt the water. "Should be warmer." She turned a faucet and sampled the water again, and then stepped into the spray and steam, hugged him, pressing her body up against his. "I have missed you. Where have you been? Where did you go? I want you to come back."

They left the shower, dried, and went to the chaise longue. She got beneath a comforter while he lit a fire and then joined her. After making love, they lay on the chaise longue. He still twitched and itched.

She said, "I think I can do it... I think I can pose for the statue."

"You're kidding. Really?"

She nodded yes.

Her acceptance came as a shock and he was stunned. He stopped breathing and felt that his heart might have stopped as well. He became dizzy, and then everything started again, as though his entire body had rebooted itself. He felt different. The twitches were gone. The cloud over his life lifted and there was relief, happiness, and even joy. He laughed aloud.

"What is the next step?" she asked.

"To visit Feo in his studio."

***

Now, the same night of their first visit to Feo's studio, where he touched her while James watched, boiling with jealousy, she sat alone in the loft at James' home with her laptop open and on, musing over the Shower of Mortification and her recovery from the trauma of it. She worried about the new strange sensations this next chapter of her life with James and Feo would reveal, but she also had a sense of what drove them to pursue the statue. She typed into shards words that feebly describe this drive.

It's a mystery buried in the alluvial layers of our minds, each layer an evolutionary step of life, each conscious of its own particular task. They send messages to the centers of our thoughts, and create urges, and pangs and mood altering chemicals that singe the linings of our hearts and steer us this way and that. This particular layer, the layer of love and pleasure, has intertwined itself with the infinitely complex and ultimately unknowable synapse network of our minds. There is no escape from it. I must sacrifice myself to it, out of my love and desire for him and his for me.

She re-read what she had written. The words soothed her and allowed her to surrender to the statue and the trepidation over Feo's touching of her so he could capture her love for James and his for her, permanently, in stone for all time.

www.ingramcontent.com/pod-product-compliance
Lightning Source LLC
Chambersburg PA
CBHW050728250626
47155CB00005B/1715